LADIES OF THE NIGHT

LADIES OF THE NIGHT

SHORT STORIES BY MAGGIE MCNEILL

---------------First Edition, January 2014---------------

Most of the stories within previously appeared in *The Honest Courtesan* (http://maggiemcneill.wordpress.com/) on the following dates: "Pandora" (October 17th-19th, 2012); "A Decent Boldness" (June 28th, 2011); "A Haughty Spirit" (June 15th, 2012); "Glorious Gifts" (June 14th, 2013); "Dry Spell" (October 13th, 2010); "Spring Forward" (March 13th, 2011); "Ripper" (November 15th, 2010); "Dance of the Seasons" (September 22nd, 2011); "Ambition" (December 22nd, 2011); "The Trick" (July 19th, 2010); "Concubine" (July 19th, 2011); "Fair Game" (May 15th, 2013); "Bucket List" (January 15th, 2013); "Mercy" (March 15th, 2013); "Bad News" (November 20th, 2011); "Empathy" (July 19th, 2012); "Carnival" (February 25th, 2011); "Friend" (August 23rd, 2012); "Genius Loci" (April 15th, 2013); "Palindrome" (January 16th, 2012); "Rose" (September 16th, 2013); "Painted Devil" (August 23rd, 2010); "Pearls Before Swine" (October 13th, 2011); "The Screening" (November 16th, 2012); "Penelope" (March 11th, 2012); "Ghost in the Machine" (August 23rd, 2011); "Faerie Tale" (April 21st, 2011); "The Specialist" (January 21st, 2011); "The Other Side" (November 15th, 2013); "For I Have Sinned" (July 15th, 2013); "Necessity" (May 24th, 2011); "X Factor" (August 15th, 2013); "Companion" (February 13th, 2012); "Monopoly" (October 15th, 2013); "Vocation" (May 11th, 2012); and "Visions of Sugarplums" (December 18th, 2012). "Nephil" is new for this collection.

This is a work of fiction. Names, characters, places and situations are either the products of the author's imagination, or are used fictitiously. Any similarity to actual events or persons living, dead or undead is entirely coincidental.

First Edition, January 2014
ISBN 1-494370-70-0
Printed in the United States of America
http://maggiemcneill.wordpress.com/

For all the great writers who inspired it; for the fifth-grade teacher who encouraged my first efforts; for the husband who supported me so I could invest the time in it; and for the readers who insisted it was good enough to publish.

Table of Contents

Ladies of the Night

Foreword

I have often said that while my Muse of Nonfiction is always amenable and eager to help me, my Muse of Fiction is like a sulky girlfriend: when she wants me she demands my immediate and undivided attention, but when she *doesn't* want me I can't even get her on the phone. However, a little over three years ago I discovered that I could win her cooperation much more dependably by the simple expedient of writing about something she found interesting…and apparently, what she finds most interesting is women who sell sex. Harlots. Whores. Prostitutes. *Demimondaines*. Doxies. Ladies of the Night, as the title promises.

This doesn't mean that the stories herein are erotica; few of them are even *erotic*, much less erotica, and neither of the two (very short) sex scenes in the entire book are depicted more graphically than one might expect in a story written a hundred years ago. The selections are mostly fantasy, science fiction and horror (hence a second meaning for the title), and you'll find most of the sex-working protagonists or antagonists aren't all that different from the characters you might find in other imaginative tales. That is to say, what makes them interesting and worth writing (or reading) about isn't bound up entirely in the fact that they sell sex, any more than any other female character's interest is entirely bound up in the fact that she's a schoolteacher, secretary, sociologist, spy or snake charmer. Some of them (such as those you'll meet in "The Trick", "Empathy" and "Faerie Tale") merely use prostitution as a means to an end, while for others (the protagonists of "Mercy", "Necessity" and "Vocation", for example) it is their life's work. But for most it's a job, neither more or less than any

Ladies of the Night

other; in a few cases I could've probably changed the profession (or not mentioned it) without much changing anything, and in three of them ("Pandora", "Rose" and "Nephil") there is no connection of any kind to what is usually considered sex work.

Now, this unifying theme is not indicative of mere academic, clinical or sexual interest on my part; I was a stripper from 1997-1999, a call girl from 2000-2006 and owned an escort service for much of that time. I was fascinated by the history and lore of the profession from my early teens, and engaged in what the literature calls "casual prostitution" whenever I was short of funds in my university days. So it surprised almost none of my friends when I went into sex work full-time after a librarian's income proved insufficient, and nobody at all when I started writing my blog, *The Honest Courtesan*, a few years after retiring from it. Though that blog ranges widely over the "realities, myths, history, lore, science, philosophy, art and every other aspect of prostitution" (as my bio puts it), it does have one unifying theme: demonstrating to readers that women who choose to sell sex are not distinctively different from other women. There is no specific "hooker type"; some of us are bold and some shy, some calculating and some sensitive, some brilliant and others rather slow, some golden-hearted and some wicked, some ambitious and some lazy. We're not all criminals, victims, homewreckers, nymphomaniacs, angels or succubae; we're just people, making a living by the means we find most effective, whether the rulers of the societies in which we live approve or not. And in their portrayal of many different kinds of women who mostly have that one single thing in common, these tales also work to demonstrate that while (I hope) also fulfilling a tale's most important function: to entertain the reader.

Foreword

Ladies of the Night

This story differs from the bulk of the collection in two major ways: it's about three times as long, and its heroine is not technically a harlot. I wrote it in the spring of 2010, just a few months before starting my blog, but it's based on a dream I had many years earlier which has never stopped haunting me; I hope it has the same effect on you. In a good way, of course.

Pandora

"Does it count as a recurring dream if only the setting stays the same?" she asked.

"I'm not sure what you mean," her husband said over his newspaper. "Everybody has dreams that take place in certain familiar places, like the house they grew up in."

"This is different," she said. "This isn't any real place I've ever been; it's like a strange city buried deep underground. All the streets are just big halls, and the houses are mostly sets of rooms cut into the stone."

"Like caves?" he asked, putting the paper aside and holding out his cup for a refill.

"No, not really," she said as she poured him more coffee. "They look just like normal houses inside, with regular rooms and straight, square, paneled walls. Sometimes the floors are bare stone, but sometimes they have rugs or even hardwood floors. The only thing out of the ordinary is that there are no windows, except on the side they face into the street."

"You mean hall."

"Well, yes, but they're *used* as though they were streets. I mean they're public places, and people come and go freely down them, whereas the houses are private places with doors that lock and belong to the people who live in them. I think."

"Are there cars in the streets, too?" he asked, seeming genuinely interested.

"No, there aren't any cars, nor machines of any kind. I mean there are simple machines, but not modern machines like cars and radios and electric light. It's kind of a medieval-type place, but clean and…" – she struggled to find the right word - "…I don't know, middle-class I guess."

"Like an underground medieval suburb?" he laughed.

"No, silly," she smiled, realizing how absurd it sounded. "I just mean it isn't filthy and poor, with a bunch of one-room hovels full of miserable people eating black bread and gruel. The houses are spacious and well-decorated, and the people are healthy and happy and have plenty to eat; it's just that they don't have modern technology."

"It sounds to me as though you've been reading too many fairy tales," he said teasingly, rising from the table. "You should be glad you live in a modern age with labor-saving conveniences that give you the time to read; women in those days had a lot more work."

"Well, they had servants too," she said, following him to the door with his coat and hat. "At least, middle and upper-class people did. I read somewhere that men in preindustrial societies actually worked *fewer* hours than most men do now, and women worked about the same unless they were lower-class or pioneers or something."

"And speaking of work," he said, "I'll be late if I don't get moving. I'll see you tonight, beautiful dreamer." She put her arms around his neck and stood on tiptoe to kiss him, then waved as he set off down the block to the train station.

But afterward, she realized that he hadn't answered the question.

That night, she walked the streets of the strange city again; it was pretty, but not fantastic. The architecture seemed real and practical, rather than ethereal and achingly beautiful like the illustrations in magazines. The designs were intended to please the eye and create light, airy spaces in what was essentially a cavern, a place which would otherwise be unfit for healthy human habitation. For there *was* light; it came down from far above, and was bright enough that she couldn't look into it, and natural enough to sustain beds of flowers and even a few ornamental shrubs here and there. One tower (a true freestanding tower rather than something cut from the rock) was even covered with ivy. The air was sweet and pure, though it did have a slight staleness which, she thought, was only natural for a place so far underground. She knew that as surely as if she could see it; this place, this city, lay buried deep in the earth under miles of rock, with no obvious connection to the surface at all.

Nobody seemed to mind, though. She walked through a lovely little cobblestoned square with a fountain in its center, and laughing children playing hide and seek while nearby adults chatted or carried packages or tended small garden plots; in the distance she could hear a dog barking, and behind a wall the sound of a hammer striking metal. A few red chickens chased insects across the paving-stones, and a cat perched like a sphinx on the edge of the fountain and regarded her with quiet curiosity. She sat down near it, and it moved a little so that she would not be quite so near and shifted its attention to the chickens. She looked down at the cobblestones, worn smooth by the passage of countless feet over what must have been many centuries; how old was this place? The edge of the fountain was in good repair, but clearly exceedingly ancient; the fountain itself was if anything older still, but in the absence of the elements which would weather stone in the surface world, the marble nymph was able to conceal her true age most enviably.

She looked at her hands; they were as soft as those in her waking life, with no sign of the calloused dryness which betokened a life of toil. Her nails were well-manicured, and her wedding ring occupied its accustomed place on her hand. Her dress was of several layers of sheer silk, thick enough for modesty yet light and cool, and her slippers were far too delicate for walking on anything rougher than pavement. So her condition in this dream-world was certainly no worse than that in waking life, and the people she encountered smiled or waved as though they knew her.

But with the realization that she was dreaming, the scene vanished like a soap bubble and she awakened in the warm darkness of her own bed. Her husband shifted restlessly, no doubt disturbed slightly by the slight start of her awakening. So she lay quietly so as to avoid arousing him completely, and though it took a very long time she eventually drifted back to sleep, and dreamt no more of the strange city that night...or if she did, she did not remember it.

"Are you sure you're awake?" he asked. "That's the third time I've asked where the butter is." She suddenly realized that he was standing in the kitchen door rather than sitting at the table as he had been; she realized guiltily that he must've asked for the butter once or twice and then gone to fetch it himself when she had failed to respond.

"I'm so sorry, darling," she said, then "sit down and I'll get it for you."

As she placed it on the table before him he asked, "Didn't you sleep well last night?"

Pandora

"Oh, it's just that dream again," she said in an annoyed tone. "It's just so clear and intense, that I have trouble getting it out of my head."

"If you have a nightmare you should wake me up," he said sympathetically, placing his hand on hers. "You know I wouldn't mind."

"But that's just it, it isn't a nightmare. Like I was trying to tell you yesterday, what happens in the dream is always different; it's only the setting that's the same."

"The underground city?"

"Yes. All sorts of different things happen, but never anything scary; it's only that the setting is so strange, and so incredibly detailed."

"Do all of your dreams take place there?"

"Oh, no, not at all; I have lots of regular dreams as well. Sometimes I go weeks without having one that takes place there, but it always eventually comes back, and much more frequently now."

"Now? How long have you been having these dreams?"

"For years now, at least since we've been married. But they used to be pretty rare, until the past few months when they started to come more frequently."

"Honey, is something wrong? Are you unhappy?" She could see he was genuinely concerned.

"Oh, no, nothing like that!" she reassured him. "I'm not at all unhappy, and I don't know why I keep having them; they don't seem to relate to anything going on in my life."

"Well, you should try to put them out of your mind, at least when you're occupied with other things," he said gently.

Ladies of the Night

"It wouldn't do for my little one to burn herself or trip and fall because her mind is somewhere else."

"You're right, of course; maybe it would help if I told you the dreams when I have them. But I just feel so damned silly."

"If it helps, tell them by all means," he said. "Anything to ensure you get your beauty sleep." She assured him she would report the next such dream, and after he left for the day she found more than enough to occupy her time and attention, and thought no more that day about the strange buried city.

It was a few days later that she once again found herself there, this time in a huge public plaza whose smallest corner could have accommodated the little fountain square and still had room for a respectable-sized pub. Its pavement was smooth, laid with tabletop-sized grey flagstones fit tightly together, and it was bounded on the longest side with what looked like a cathedral. Several streets entered at corners of the irregularly-shaped space, and except for a lovely arcade down one side the other walls of the plaza were occupied by various places of business. The open area was crowded with stalls from which merchants hawked a variety of wares and bargained with frugal housewives; the noise was incredible, the clothes were of every hue imaginable and the smells ranged from sickening to mouth-watering. She moved down the lanes between the stalls, taking in the sights, examining the merchandise, and tasting samples when they were offered. Sometimes she was jostled, sometimes looked over by young men, and once a little girl of about six tugged on her skirt, obviously having mistaken her for a similarly-dressed mother or aunt. And as always before, despite the

Pandora

exotic surroundings there was a strange familiarity about the place; people greeted her as if they either knew her or had seen her around town, and she had no trouble finding her way about any part of the city she had ever visited.

After a little while she decided to seek a quieter neighborhood and so turned into the nearest street, which happened to be the one directly across from the cathedral. It was much wider than the other streets and clearly less travelled; in fact, despite its connection to the crowded marketplace, she soon found herself walking completely alone past oddly featureless walls. Before too long the street ended at a very large and heavily-barred door; two narrow streets ran out from the portal at forty-five degree angles from the wide avenue by which she approached, and a glance down these alleys led her to the realization that except for the door itself, the wall ahead of her was absolutely featureless. No ornamentation or stonework bounded it, and as far as the eye could see in either direction the wall ran smooth and unbroken by window, seam or sculpture until it vanished around a bend.

Even in a city so clearly marked by age, the door positively radiated antiquity; the dry atmosphere had preserved the ancient wood long past the epoch in which it would have rotted away in natural weather. The bar was topped with a thick film of dust, and the iron fittings looked as though they had been forged in the morning of the world. And for the first time since she had been coming to the city she was afraid; something about this silent barrier terrified her, and she withdrew her hand and began to back away, her eyes fixed on it as though she expected it to burst open. But before she had taken seven steps back a hand fell on her shoulder, and though the voice which said "you know you shouldn't be here, Miss" was not unkind, and the eyes of the old guardsman gentle, she awoke in a paroxysm of terror and screamed aloud.

"You gave me quite a scare last night, dear one," he said, caressing her hair as they lay in bed. "Do you feel up to talking about it now?"

She pulled herself a little closer to his chest. "I feel like such a fool, screaming like that! Like a stupid little girl, afraid of shadows!"

"It's not foolish to be afraid of nightmares," he said. "Everyone has them occasionally."

"But that's just it, it wasn't a nightmare! At least, not at first; it was just the usual kind of dream of the underground city, with absolutely nothing to be afraid of."

"But clearly, something changed; you were never scared by a dream like that before, not enough to wake up screaming anyway."

"But there was nothing to be afraid of," she repeated. There was a moment of silence, and though she couldn't see his face she knew he was waiting for her to continue. He had accepted her unwillingness to discuss it in the middle of the night, had simply whispered words of reassurance and held her while she cried. But she couldn't very well refuse to tell him now; she had agreed to share the dreams with him, and her reason told her that the fantasies of sleep were nothing to fear in the light of day. Yet she couldn't tell him about the awful door and the inexplicable terror it had evoked in her; how does one explain such a thing? He would worry that it was a sign of some deep emotional disturbance, might even be upset at his inability to protect her from her own irrational fears. So she stammered out some half-truths about going someplace in the city she shouldn't have gone, and being surprised by the guard. If he doubted her veracity he gave no sign, merely held her closer for awhile and then began to make small-talk about ordinary things.

He didn't have to work that day, so they spent it together; they went for a walk in the park, then to one of their favorite restaurants for dinner, and he took her to a show. It was a comedy, and though she laughed as much as anyone she could not completely forget the terror of the previous night.

The dreams became more frequent now, and subtly different; though the city had not changed her feelings about it had. The scenes and the people were as before, but she couldn't help looking up at the artificial "sky" and thinking obsessively about the incalculable tons of rock overhead; what once had seemed a sanctuary now felt like a tomb, and she began to wonder why these people had sealed themselves off from heaven for uncounted generations. And more and more she found herself visiting the door, which though it had not ceased to frighten her yet gripped her in a terrible fascination. She did not repeat her mistake of the first time; she quickly learned the routine of the guards, and made sure she never paused in the area when they were about. For strangely enough, no one else seemed affected by the door as she was; if they thought about it at all it must have been with an unswerving confidence that it would continue to keep out whatever was beyond it as it always had. The guards were all old, and none of them but the one she had encountered on her first visit seemed even remotely concerned with the possibility that anyone would tamper with the ancient portal in even the most superficial fashion.

She had stopped telling her husband about the dreams; he asked a few times in the next several months, and though she did not lie outright she downplayed both their importance and their frequency. Either he believed her or he realized there was nothing he could really say, for it eventually ceased to be a topic of conversation. She had become very good at putting them out of her mind when he was home; she was reasonably sure that her behavior was not any different from what it always had been, and that no moodiness betrayed her secret to him. And she had plenty of practice, for she eventually began to dream of the city every night.

Then one day she arose early to get a head start on some major housecleaning she wanted to do; the work went more smoothly than expected, however, and she found herself done by mid-afternoon, but unusually tired from hard work performed after less sleep than usual. She therefore decided to take a nap, and soon found herself in the city again. But this time something was noticeably different; the overhead light which had never before varied in intensity was now very dim, almost completely dark in fact, and there was not a soul abroad on the streets. At first she was at a loss to understand what had happened, then she realized the truth: In order to maintain the health and sanity of the citizenry, darkness was periodically created by somehow dimming or shuttering the mysterious source of "sunlight." For the first time, she was in the city at night, and though the reason she had never before observed this phenomenon did not occur to her during the visit, it was obvious when she awoke: She was not in the habit of taking afternoon naps. The day and

Pandora

night of the underground city were the opposite of those in the waking world, so that it was awake while she slept and slept during the day, when she was normally awake. And with this realization was born a plan, a means by which she might finally satisfy her burning curiosity as to what lay beyond the sealed portal and why the people of the city lived as they did, forever hidden from sun and sky.

It was quite simple, really; when she visited the city that night she bought a black cloak from one of the merchants in the plaza, and hid it in a large, empty urn on one of the less frequented streets near the door. She did not know if she had a residence in the city; if she had, she could not recall ever having been there. Her clothes were different in each visit, but she seemed to have no conscious control over what she would be wearing when she found herself there, nor any recollection of getting dressed. But given the uncanny consistency of her dreams of the city, and the near-abandoned state of the quarter near the door, she felt sure the cloak would still be there when next she visited. After that, it was merely a matter of getting up early the next morning and working hard all day so as to be tired enough for an afternoon nap.

Once again she found herself in a quiet, darkened city; she retraced her steps to the hiding place and there was her cloak, exactly as she had left it. It provided her perfect camouflage for skulking about the darkened streets, and in a few minutes she carefully approached her goal, confident that if a guard was near he was probably napping rather than diligently scanning the empty streets for moving shadows. It never occurred to her that the bar would be immovable; perhaps it was somehow maintained, or that the antediluvian architects who designed it knew engineering secrets long since forgotten, or that some force wished her to succeed; perhaps it is merely due to the fact that some things which are impossible in waking life come easily in dreams. But in any case the enormous bar slid aside as though moved by a well-oiled machine, and with no more sound than a rusty hinge might make. A quick look around assured her that no one had heard the brief noise, and the creak of the ponderous door was no louder; she opened it just enough to admit her through the gap, and was through in another moment.

The room beyond was suffused by the same dim, shadowy light as was the rest of the sleeping city, but it was enough to reveal her surroundings; she was at the bottom of an enormous square stairwell, and above her a wooden stairway, clearly of the same era as the door, stretched up flight after flight, circling the interior of the stairwell, until it was lost in the gloom above.

She wanted to start up the stairs immediately, but realized it would be a mistake to do so now; though she had long since learned to stay asleep no matter what she saw or experienced in the city, she was sure that her husband could still awaken her if he came home to find her still napping. Besides, she was not exactly dressed for this sort of excursion, and what if a section of the stairs far above had collapsed or been otherwise rendered impassible? She had come too far to ruin everything by impatience, so she slipped back through the door and closed it. The bar offered far more resistance in closing than in opening, but after several tense minutes of struggle she at last succeeded in sliding it back to its original position. She then returned her cloak to its hiding place and willed herself to awaken.

Pandora

The evening passed with aching slowness; she wanted nothing more than to go to bed so she could finally see the end of the whole weird business. The dream-world had become so real to her, so important, that it was beginning to feel more real to her than waking life; she could remember the events of her dreams with crystal clarity, but real-life events had begun to grow fuzzy and hard to remember from day to day. Her husband repeatedly asked if she was sleeping well, and had even suggested she see a doctor; she knew that his suggestions would soon turn to insistence if things continued this way for even a few more days. But she was absolutely positive that tonight would see a resolution; she knew that as soon as she reached the top of those stairs, the greatest mystery of her life would be solved and everything would fall into place. She would return to the happy life she had once known and again be able to devote herself to her wonderful husband, the man who had loved her and cared for her and tolerated her shortcomings with rarely more than a cross word. So she made a supreme effort to be pleasant and engaging and fun this evening, while secretly counting the minutes until bedtime.

Once they were in bed she offered herself to him, and as he made love to her she thought how this, too had changed. Once she had looked forward to their time together, had lost herself in his embrace; in the past few months, however, she had found it impossible to stop thinking of the buried city even while with him, and it had become merely a duty to her. Oh, she had pretended of course, in order to spare his feelings, but she sorely missed the true physical intimacy that had once come so naturally to her in his arms. After tonight, she told herself, this, too would return to normal.

As soon as he was asleep she set out for the marketplace, where she bought a pair of trousers and some sturdy boots, then a set of the odd claw-like appliances which she had once seen a man use to scale the cathedral's steeple in order to effect some maintenance. She doubted she could use them with anything like the agility displayed by that worker, but she would only need them if she had to climb over some bad spot on the immense staircase. The merchant looked at her strangely when she requested the items, but asked no questions and simply handed them over once she had paid the requested price. Her next stop was the hiding-place of her cloak, and thence to a spot where she could wait until the guard had passed in his rounds.

Once he had passed she flew to the door and slid back the bar; it moved just as smoothly as it had the previous night, and with less noise. A moment more and she was through the door; this time she closed it, hoping that the drawn bar would escape notice for long enough for her to ascend out of reach of any pursuit. Gathering her skirt with her free hand, she took the steps as quickly as she dared, stopping eight flights up – that is, two complete circuits of the stairwell – to replace skirt with trousers and slippers with boots. She paused to look and listen for long enough to satisfy herself that her trespass had not yet been detected, then donned her cloak and set out to make the arduous climb.

She was careful to pace herself; there was no way of knowing how high the staircase was, since its top was lost in the gloom. Though the city was brightly lit by day, the staircase was wrapped in the same shadowy light by which she had first seen it last night. After a while she grew tired of carrying her skirt and slippers and so discarded them; she then donned the climbing appliances under the assumption that they would be less cumbersome worn than carried. Hour after hour she climbed, until her legs screamed in protest and her lungs ached with the unaccustomed effort, but still the impossible stairway stretched above her, flight upon flight upon endless flight. At first she tried to count them, but lost track somewhere above five hundred; she must now be miles above the city. She moved like an automaton, her agony conquered by the overwhelming determination to reach the top no matter how long it took or what it did to her body.

After what seemed an eternity, she came to the sudden realization that the echoes of her plodding footsteps sounded different somehow; without stopping, she veered toward the railing so she could look up for the first time in hours, and her heart leapt as she saw the unmistakable outline of a peaked roof some ten flights above her. Though she had awakened from the trance-like stupor in which she had climbed for a very long time, the anticipation of reaching the top at last allowed her to force the pain back down and continue climbing.

She had cleared four more flights when she heard an ominous boom from above, like the slamming of a massive door, and a shock of terror ripped through her when it was followed by a sound which could only be heavy footfalls coming down the staircase toward her. She came very close to blind panic at that moment; the idea that the top of the stairway might be guarded like the bottom had never entered her mind. But somehow she found the calm center of the emotional storm which threatened to engulf her, and looked down at the climbing appliances strapped to her hands and

Ladies of the Night

boots. She gambled a quick look up the stairwell to make sure that the unknown intruder was not in sight of the edge, then swung herself out over the railing and climbed along the underside of the wooden steps until she could rest against the wall in a desperate effort to conserve what little strength she had left.

Her cloak now hung uncomfortably from her neck, but she dared not remove and drop it for fear that it would land on the stairs below and thereby draw the climber's attention upward when he passed below her. So she waited and waited, her heart pounding against the inside of her ribs, as the footfalls came closer and closer and ever closer...and stopped directly above her.

She began to weep silently, and held her breath so as to suppress any sniffle or sob which might betray her presence, but it was obviously too late; it was not by accident that the other had stopped where he did. As she looked out from her hiding place, hoping against hope that the descent would resume, a long, rough-skinned neck as thick as her waist and the color of dried blood came curling down from the stairs above; it was surmounted by a reptilian head the size of a tiger's, and as she watched in helpless terror the monstrosity turned its head completely around on its neck and stared at her with huge, glowing green eyes. Its lower jaw fell open as if unhinged, revealing many sharp teeth accented by four prominent fangs shaped like those of a cobra, and it emitted a hiss more like steam escaping from a pipe than anything a living creature might make. Her nerve shattered completely, and she screamed and let go of her precarious perch, dropping heavily to the stairs beneath.

It was difficult to see the hideous thing clearly from her new position, but the green glow of its eyes stood out in the gloom. Oddly, it hesitated for a moment, and that gave her enough time to rise to her tortured legs and begin to run downward, back the way she had come. Her headlong flight appeared to incense the creature, and it began to run down the stairway after her. Even in her profound horror she realized that it would be impossible to outrun the monster; not only were its strides worth three of hers, it was fresh from descending only a few flights while she was absolutely spent from her ascent of hundreds. Whether by intuition or reason or pure repetition, she swung out over the edge of the staircase again in the wild hope that it might overlook the possibility of her pulling the same trick twice. And by some miracle it worked; the loathsome thing was so caught up in the pursuit that it shot past above and then below her without as much as a glance in her direction. As soon as it turned the corner below her she scrambled up onto the stairs again, taking the steps as quickly as her ruined legs would carry her, and threw open the door at the top of the stairs without breaking her stride.

She instantly found herself lying in her own bed, her legs twisted with cramps, and burst into tears born from a mixture of fear and relief. She clutched at her husband and he turned to hold her gently, then with infinite sadness he asked, "Why did you have to go through the door?" But she was unable to answer; she merely stared in mute horror at his eyes glowing green in the dark.

Ladies of the Night

The next three stories are about Aella, a young Amazon warrior of the mythic past. I envision her world as something like Robert E. Howard's Hyborian Age, lying "…Between the years when the oceans drank Atlantis and the gleaming cities, and the years of the rise of the Sons of Aryas…" Aella is the only character who appears more than once in this book; when I published "A Decent Boldness" in June of 2011 my readers insisted I let her tell more of her story, so she returned again in June of 2012 and 2013, and for all I know may pop up again.

A Decent Boldness

A decent boldness ever meets with friends. -
Homer, *Odyssey* (VII, 67)

Tartessos. By Theia, what a dump.

I suppose it was my own fault; I should've known
better than to trust Derinoe. She was always restless,
constantly talking about leaving Amazonia to see Man's
World before being tied down with children and a farm.
Besides, she pointed out, in peacetime there wasn't exactly
any way for us to distinguish ourselves as warriors, which
meant that we'd either be stuck tilling our mothers' fields or
having to endure the back-breaking labor of clearing new
land without slaves, since we had neither war in which to
capture them nor money with which to buy them from the
traders. And though I couldn't argue with any of that,
something told me that signing on as mercenaries to fight in a
war at (literally) the edge of the world probably wasn't an
idea which came straight from Metis. Yet I ignored my
misgivings and let Derinoe fill my head full of stories about
the Silver Kingdom and the riches we were sure to win.

So now I'm stranded among barbarians with neither
money nor food nor knowledge of the gibberish they speak in
this benighted land; Derinoe and the others are all dead, and I
haven't the faintest clue of how to get home even if I cared to
endure months of travel on one of those awful galleys (a
method of transportation so dangerous and uncomfortable
only a man could've invented it), which I most certainly
don't. Riding the whole way would be out of the question
even if I *had* a horse, because all I know is that Amazonia
lies in the direction of the sunrise and that nearly every nation

25

Ladies of the Night

between here and Colchis is hostile; though I trust my skill with sword and bow, I also know the difference between confidence and suicide.

If I were still a girl I would cry, but I'm a grown woman of seventeen and our goddesses expect Amazon warriors to have courage in the face of adversity. I can't just sit here feeling sorry for myself and dwelling on my misfortunes; I need to take stock of my assets. Let's see; my wounds are quite minor, my helmet and shield are undamaged and my sword is vastly superior to any of the crude excuses for weapons I've seen in the past few months. My bow is in good condition and I still have (six, seven) eight arrows before I have to start hunting materials to make more, which won't be easy in a city (assets, now, not liabilities!) And I have the protective talisman my mother gave me before I left. Oh, and when fighting men I have the advantage of surprise because they expect me to be as soft and useless as these frail Western wenches.

But that's about it. And I'm hungry now. I can hear the noises of the marketplace from here, and though I'm sure I could probably steal a melon or a loaf of bread I won't disgrace Amazon honor by stooping to common thievery; I'll just have to hike out of the city and carefully stalk some game. That'll give me food for at least a few meals, assuming I can find something bigger than a rabbit or one of these filthy sea birds that foul this whole city with their noisome droppings. There now, that's a plan at last, thank Metis! Now to figure out which is the quickest way out of town; I think if I follow this large and well-travelled road from the marketplace I'm bound to come to a gate sooner rather than later.

How now, what *is* that racket? Even in a place where people habitually shout at one another, that sounds like trouble. Well, it won't hurt to take a look and…NO! I know these people's ways are different from ours, but this just *can't* be right; this girl is no warrior, yet a man beats her as one would beat a dog who had stolen sausages. By Themis, I cannot ignore this! It's over in an instant; the drunken fool never hears my approach, and before he can strike the terrified girl twice more I lay him low with a sharp blow to his head from the edge of my shield. As he collapses to the ground, his victim's eyes grow wide and she looks back and forth from him to me as if she doubts the evidence of her senses.

Within moments, I am surrounded by other women, chattering like a pack of squirrels in their incomprehensible gobbledygook. They're pointing at my weapons and looking at my fallen foe, and though I can tell from their inflections they're asking me questions I just shake my head and hold my arms wide in exasperation. Suddenly, out of the meaningless sounds I hear a few recognizable words; they are spoken in the tongue of Crete, whose people come often to our land to trade! I immediately turn to the woman who spoke them and let her know that I understand her. The others quickly grow quiet, and she says that the women are grateful to me for saving their friend and that they wish me to stay for dinner.

As my interpreter conducts me inside, she tells me (I think) that her education enabled her to guess my race, and she asks how I came to be so far from my native shores. I explain as best I can in my limited command of her tongue, and she repeats it in Tarshi to their captain, to whom I have been presented. Before long we eat, and though the Cretan woman tries to explain what kind of place this is, and why

Ladies of the Night

the man was assaulting the hapless girl, I am not quite sure
that I understand. There is no word in the Amazon language
to name this place or the trade of those who live here, and
when she eventually gets me to understand that men pay
these women generously just to mate with them for an hour I
decide that the men of the Outer World are all quite mad.
But mad or not, I exclaim a prayer of thanksgiving when the
Cretan, on instruction from her captain, offers me
employment here as a guard at a wage *five times* that I was
promised as a mercenary!

  Later that evening, my belly full, I do my best to learn
a few words of their babble while on duty in the atrium,
watching the women's customers come and go; only once are
my services needed, and even then my scowling presence is
enough to cow the fat little man into what I take to be an
apology to the woman he had apparently threatened. The
Cretan has apparently been assigned to teach me, for she
remains with me all night and patiently explains (through
constant repetition and rephrasing until I understand) some of
the strange things that men pay the girls for beside mating.
She even tells me that tomorrow I will be paid a bonus equal
to half of my daily wages if I agree to whip a customer as one
whips a disobedient slave, in other words to hurt but not
injure. Obviously I must not understand correctly; I'm sure
I'll grasp it better when the time comes. But one thing is for
certain: in spite of herself, poor Derinoe set me on the right
track after all. In a few years I will be able to return home far
wealthier than most women my age, without having to live in
filthy camps or face death every day to accomplish it.

A Haughty Spirit

Do thou restrain the haughty spirit in thy breast, for better far is gentle courtesy. - Homer, *Iliad* (IX, 315-317)

Hecate take me for my damnable overconfidence!

Phaedra wanted to go by ship, but I said no, I hate the cursed things, and though your home be on an island I want to make as much of the journey safely on land as possible. My four years at the brothel had allowed me to earn not only wealth, but also knowledge; once word of my presence got around Tartessos a group of kindly scholars began to frequent the place, and I was as interested in learning from them as they were from me. When I heard that the ancient homeland of my people lay just on the other side of the Pillars of Herakles, I yearned to visit it before returning to our modern domain on the eastern shores of Tethys; and truth be told, had I not had that excuse I would have found another to avoid being cooped up for weeks in close quarters on a frail thing of wood with a lot of rude, smelly men.

I convinced her to ride with me as far as Rehoboth or Graea, where we could surely book a comparatively-short passage to Crete; I painted a lovely picture of riding along beaches, eating fish and crabs from the sea with the good wine and cheese we brought along, sleeping beneath the stars and sharing laughter and kisses away from the prying eyes of crowds. I dismissed her concerns of dangerous beasts and even more dangerous tribes, boasting of my ability to defeat man or lion. Eventually she agreed, and the first two weeks were just as I promised.

And now here I lie, gazing helplessly into the barbarian camp where my dearest friend awaits rape, slavery

Ladies of the Night

and perhaps torture, and it's all my fault! Why did I leave her alone while I explored those ruins? My time in the soft city has dulled my wits and clouded my judgment, and I forgot that in the wilderness there is too much danger to leave a girl like Phaedra for long without a vigilant sword at her side. Damn you, eyes, for these annoying tears! I need you clear that I may assess the situation, hopeless though it may be; I doubt even Queen Myrina and her honor guard could slay so many men without being overwhelmed. So if Amazon steel will not serve me, perhaps a warrior's cunning will; Metis, inspire me with a plan!

What's this? Though I did not see her brought hither, my time in Man's World has taught me enough to know the chief will have claimed her for himself, and there is some kind of ruckus at his tent. Though their babble is as strange to me as Tarshi once was, an argument sounds the same in any tongue…and one that ends with a sword through the gut is serious indeed. But what could spur a leader to kill his own man so abruptly? Did he attempt to steal treasure? Ah, I know; he attempted to *sample* treasure, or at least the chief thought he did. Phaedra is very beautiful, and he wishes to keep her all to himself; though there are already many women in the camp, her fair skin and shining grey eyes make her unique. And that gives me an idea; may my ancestresses forgive me, but I can think of no other way.

First, I must prepare our escape; would that I could find and extract Phaedra as easily as I locate our horses among these inferior nags! The rest of the camp is at dinner, and the guard is inattentive; may Themis be more merciful to his soul than his people were to my friend. If I leave the paddock gate open, some of the horses may wander away now and bolt if any commotion starts, and that will mean fewer pursuers. Fortunately, this terrain provides plenty of

30

A Haughty Spirit

cover behind which to secure our mounts. My helm, shield,
breastplate and greaves need be packed away, and my sword,
bow and quiver will hang from the pommel securely enough;
my face, my wits and a long dagger strapped to my thigh will
be my only weapons this night, and my mother's talisman
and the grace of the blessed goddesses my only armor. They
have already granted me one boon: though the barbarians
stole woman and horses, they missed our packs where we had
wedged them between rocks to protect them from the
blowing dust.

    Now for the hard part: though it is a good thing
Phoebe will not rise for hours yet, it means having to find
what I need in the dark. Ah, this isn't so difficult after all;
this flimsy gown Phaedra insisted I bring to present myself at
her mother's house is so much softer to the touch than my
other clothes, I can find it with my fingers! If only the rest
could be so simple. I've been watching the way the women
of the brothel behave for four years now; have I learned
enough to imitate it? Best to test it before entering the lion's
den; here's another guard looking for the one I permanently
relieved of duty a little while ago.

    Quiet, my heart! Cease pounding so, or he will surely
hear! The dagger is within easy reach should my attempt at
seduction (what a strange word!) fail. Now to step out where
he can see me...no, mustn't strike a defensive stance! He
must think I'm just as useless as the women of his tribe.
He's suspicious; of course he is! He isn't an idiot! This is
transparently a trap, and surely no sane creature could...
sheath his sword and approach unarmed, mumbling barbarian
gibberish. A smile and a beckoning finger...and he joins his
comrade on the shores of the Styx. Perhaps my plan may

Ladies of the Night

work after all; it seems that any possibility of coupling with a woman causes these men of the West to completely take leave of their senses.

Still, there's no need to test it more than is necessary; my stealth will carry me to the leader's tent with far less chance of failure. Slit one more throat, dodge two women, hide for interminable minutes behind some jars while a group of children tarry before dispersing...then wait while a sentry moves on, and here I am at my destination. I can hear Phaedra's voice; the chief apparently knows enough Cretan to suffice for trade, and she is trying to negotiate herself out of the situation by promising a reward if he returns her to me. He seems to find it funny; has she told him I'm an Amazon? It's impossible to tell.

I want so badly to rush in and cut the dog down where he stands, but I'm no fool; as a chieftain he will be at least my equal in fair combat, and the melee will surely draw his guards. No, this has to be done with finesse...so I let the guards think they've overheard me, and pretend to be frightened (o, the humiliation!) when they "capture" me, crying out loudly enough to ensure the leader hears as well. When he steps out, I catch his eyes with as smoldering a look as I can manage...and he takes the bait, ordering his men to bring me in.

Phaedra's eyes go wide in horror, but that lasts only for a moment as I rush to her in unfeigned joy and hug her tightly, slipping my dagger from beneath my skirts and placing it between her thighs. She starts slightly, and I whisper "You'll know when" before allowing myself to be jerked around roughly by our barbaric captor. What follows is the hardest battle of my life; I have to force down my loathing, compel myself to keep smiling, to keep chatting, to somehow subtly convince him that his lust for me is greater than his lust for my beautiful friend…to succeed in a form of bloodless combat I have never before attempted.

Victory! Astarte be praised! The fool at last imposes himself on me, pushing me back upon the bedding to enter me; I distract him with a great cacophony of moans, encouraging him to ever-louder noises himself while beckoning to Phaedra for my blade. He dies with a shout indistinguishable from his other bestial noises, and I roll him off of me in disgust. Shush, my love; we must needs flee in haste and utmost silence. It is the work of a moment to slide under the back of the tent, and apparently Nike is satisfied with the four men I have already sent her this night, for we meet no more on the way to our steeds. The sun is high before we dare stop for a short rest, and has set again before we make a hidden camp far above the shore. But my exhaustion and saddle-soreness, and the cold fare on which we must dine, are all made bearable by the admiration in my dear friend's eyes, and the songs of praise that pour from her lips until I drop off into a well-earned sleep.

Ladies of the Night

Glorious Gifts

The glorious gifts of the gods are not to be cast aside. - Homer, *Iliad* (III, 65)

Asteria send me guidance tonight, for I am afraid.

I who alone of this living generation travelled West to the very end of the Earth, bathed in the waters of Keto and returned to tell the tale; I who walked in the ancient places of our people, rescued my dearest friend from the hands of barbarians and protected us both from the beasts of the wilderness; I who lived among strangers for five years and brought much of the learning of the Outer World back to the Motherland: I am more frightened than I have ever been since earning the title of warrior. For tomorrow, I must face the Council of Elders, thirteen grey old veterans of battles fought before my mother was born, and defend my conduct before them.

But for the life of me, O Blessed Goddess, I cannot fathom why what I did should have shocked the others so. True, it was a new idea, but what of that? Why was I brought home through so many dangers if not to share the knowledge and the ideas of our sisters across the sea? Harmothoe says my mind was addled by my time in Man's World, but she's simply jealous because I returned from my journey with enough wealth to buy a farm and enough slaves to work it, while she's stuck toiling on our mother's place. I offered to lend her my slaves this winter to clear new land, but that won't win her the respect and admiration I've enjoyed since my return, nor an invitation to visit the Queen's palace next month so that I can tell her of my adventures. Of course, if the hearing goes against me

Ladies of the Night

tomorrow I may see her sooner than that, though as a prisoner rather than an honored guest.

And all this fuss over something so completely stupid. Are not health, strength, beauty, wisdom and skill at arms gifts of the goddesses? And are we not to use those gifts to improve our places in the world? Don't the more beautiful and distinguished among us have greater choice among the Scythian men at the Spring Festival? After all, our Princess Penthesilia is the daughter of their King Arius, not of some lowly tradesman; our Queen sought out the best sire available when she was ready to bear the child who would succeed to her throne. And though I am not of noble blood, yet my company was highly sought by the men this year for the same reason my Amazon sisters have sought it since my return: though men and women differ in many ways, we all love a good story and many of both sexes seek to borrow prestige by association when they cannot win it for themselves.

But all that attention was a mixed blessing; with so many men competing to mate with me this year, how was I to choose one? I'm no mere girl to be impressed by a handsome face, and my experience in Man's World taught me that many a great athlete is also a great fool. I thought on this as I watched the games and partook in the feasting, and it occurred to me that the best approach would be a practical one. After all, our motives for mating with the Scythian men are wholly pragmatic in the first place; it stands to reason a pragmatic means of choosing a mate is in order as well. And one can never have too much wealth, so what could be more sensible than simply announcing that the man who gave me the most generous gift would be the one who could lie with me? I thought it was a wonderful idea, and the men responded with enthusiasm; the winner gave me six snow-

36

Glorious Gifts

white kine and an equally-beautiful bull. But to hear my sisters, one would've thought I had drunk myself silly and puked on the banquet table. The next day it was the talk of the town, and by the end of the week…well, here I am.

Goddess, I suppose You know all this already, but it never hurts to summarize; besides, I want You to understand how I saw the matter. Mother says I've disgraced our family, and Aunt Laomache says it just goes to show why Amazons shouldn't associate with outsiders any more than is strictly necessary. Granny is the only one who was helpful; she says what this demonstrates is that long periods of peace aren't good for us, because when there isn't anything real to fret about people make a big deal out of nothing, and in the absence of an actual enemy they invent imaginary bogeys to get worked up about. She also said that the council only summoned me to shut up the prattlers, and that if they were truly concerned I would be spending the night under guard rather than lying in my own bed. Also, Elder Dioxippe is Granny's best friend, and Granny told me that she had talked it over with her and at least several of the Council were equally unimpressed with the gravity of my so-called sin; she predicted they would direct me to apologize to my family and sacrifice one of the kine to Astarte, and that would be the end of it.

I certainly hope so, but I can't help worrying. And that's why I'm praying about this to You instead of Themis or Metis; there's no justice in this situation, it seems like thinking logically is what got me into this fix, and perhaps divine inspiration is what's needed to get me out. If my punishment is as light as Granny thinks it'll be, I'll make a special gift to You; I think I might have conceived by the generous one, and if it's a girl and I name her for You, she will be a constant reminder of Your grace.

And also of the fact that most people have no respect for pragmatism.

Glorious Gifts

Ladies of the Night

One thing you'll notice about my stories is that even when they take place in contemporary times, they're not always exactly contemporary; some stories in this collection take place in the early 1960s, or the '90s, or some other recent decade. Nor do I necessarily feel the need to spell it out, as you probably noticed in "Pandora". Keep that in mind as you read this one.

Dry Spell

Every once in a while, things slow down for one reason or another; we are, after all, a luxury, and if the gentlemen have pressing things they *must* spend their money on, why then they haven't got as much for things they might *like* to spend it on. Every girl who's been in this business for a couple of years learns the seasonal variations and comes to expect the periodic unpredictable ones; one develops a philosophical attitude toward it. *"To every thing there is a season, and a time to every purpose under the heaven,"* as Ecclesiastes put it. *"A time to embrace, and a time to refrain from embracing..."* that's certainly the verse that applies here. But one might wish they wouldn't refrain for quite so long. Because it has been a long dry spell indeed, probably the longest one I've ever seen.

Oh, I knew it would be when we heard about the stock market crashing on the radio; all the girls sat around listening, and though most of the younger ones didn't really understand what was happening Madam Theresa tried to explain it to them. I didn't understand it all as well as Madam did, but I knew enough to know that we were in trouble. Though she tried to hide it Madam was plenty worried; enough of her money was tied up in stocks that her financial future (and with it ours) was in considerable doubt, and since most of our clients were businessmen even the ones who *weren't* ruined were not going to have any money to spend on good-time girls for quite a while.

I wish I had been wrong, but I wasn't. Madam put on a brave face: We were all set for the "holiday slump" anyhow, she reminded us; it's just starting a few weeks early this year is all. Why, by mid-January things will start to pick

41

Ladies of the Night

up just like they always do. And though this made the young
ones feel better, one doesn't get to be top girl in a first-class
bordello without knowing how to read people; I knew that
Madam didn't believe a word she was saying. She told me in
secret that she was determined to ride this thing out and
support all the girls for as long as need be; no girl of hers was
going to be turned out on the street, she said. And I knew she
meant it, but I also knew that good intentions don't put bread
on the table.

And as the weeks became months, what was on the
table gradually dwindled to not much more than bread.
Fortunately Madam owned her house outright, but there were
taxes to be paid and bills for electricity and telephone service
and gas and water, and unlike us the staff were on salary; all
that left precious little for meat and extras. But since we had
recently taken a big shipment of imported liquor drink was
not in short supply, and it pained me to see that by springtime
Madam was rarely without a glass in her hand.

We still had a few faithful regulars; some were rich
men who passed the crisis unscathed, others had spread their
wealth more carefully than most and so were still doing all
right, and a few were in professions or owned businesses
which people always need no matter what. But even they did
not spend as freely as they once did, and though I was not
privy to Madam's business affairs I can do sums well enough
to know that she was falling behind every month. Before too
long Madam was no longer wearing some of her more
expensive jewelry, and original paintings and antique
furniture were quietly and gradually replaced by prints and
modern furniture. The less popular girls went back to their
families or took whatever menial work they could get, and
even a few of the popular girls decided they were better off
being kept by bankers or bootleggers than having to go

Dry Spell

without nice clothes and perfume. By summertime things seemed to stabilize, though at a much lower level than before; there was enough business to support the girls who were left, and though Madam couldn't have been making much I don't believe she was losing money, either. If things had stayed that way I think it would have eventually been OK, but apparently Fate had decreed otherwise.

See, up until the Crash we had a good relationship with the local mob; Madam bought their liquor and provided the bigwigs with hospitality and everyone was happy. But I guess they were hurting like most people, so they gradually started getting a lot more demanding than in the old days. Madam didn't like to air her dirty laundry in front of the girls, but I'm not deaf and gangsters aren't known for their discretion. First they took issue with our smaller liquor orders, then they wanted girls to "service" some of the lower echelons, and then they actually started demanding a cut of her nearly-nonexistent profits. Eventually things degenerated completely, and the boss left in a huff one night, yelling that Madam would soon wish she had "been smart."

Later that night I awoke to the smell of smoke and shouts of "Fire!" from downstairs; I ran down and joined our cook, Tillie, in beating it with blankets while her husband Jake, our handyman, got the water hose. It seemed to take Jake forever, and I wondered if the gangsters who had set the fire (an "accident" so soon after that warning was just too convenient to be believable) had also stolen or cut the hose. By the time he got there the whole kitchen was full of smoke and I couldn't see a thing, but eventually we did get it out (though the kitchen was utterly ruined).

Ladies of the Night

Madam had wisely continued our fire insurance even through the hard times, so it was soon repaired, yet nothing was ever the same again. It was as though the fire had burned out Madam's spirit; she started drinking again as she had right after the crash, and cried a great deal. And though she still talked to me as much as she ever had, it seemed as though she would not listen to my answers; she was lost in her own little world. While I had previously been the most popular girl in the house, now it seemed as though the clients were suddenly uninterested in me; they just passed me by, and none even wanted to talk to me. Sometimes they even got up and moved to a different part of the room when I sat down next to them; it's enough to cause a girl to seriously doubt herself. But I won't, I won't...it's just a dry spell, and it will end; they always do. *To every thing there is a season, and a time to every purpose under the heaven: A time to be born, and...and...*

"So you think this is the one?" David asked, examining the old photograph and then glancing at the typed pages in the folder. "Beatrice Elaine Becket, August 16th, 1901 to October 13th, 1931. Why her? Nobody's ever seen her clearly, after all."

"Just an educated guess," said Dr. Wayne. "Of all the former residents of this house, she's the only one known to have actually died on the premises, and the disturbances began only a few months later."

The graduate student was still leafing through the papers in the file. "So this was a whorehouse, right? And this chick was one of the whores?"

The older man frowned. "A little respect for the dead if you please, David. Yes, it was a brothel, the finest in the

Dry Spell

city in its day. But after the Crash of '29 its fortunes
dwindled, and after Beatrice's death the Madam became an
alcoholic and the place really ran down until it was closed
after a police raid in 1936."

"She was really attached to the girl, huh?"

"Yes, and blamed herself for her death. The local
crime boss was putting considerable pressure on her and she
was resisting, so they lit a fire as a warning. It was probably
just intended to scare her into capitulating but it got out of
control, and when Beatrice tried to help put it out she was
overcome by the smoke. The cook, Matilda Johnson, is still
alive; I interviewed her last week and she still cries when she
talks about that night."

"So, Doc, what do you think she wants? Revenge on
the guys who lit the fire?"

"You've been reading too many ghost stories. Look
at the facts; this is a very gentle sort of manifestation, not like
a vengeance-driven haunting at all. She usually appears as
nothing more than a warm spot or a scent of jasmine, but
some witnesses have reported a sense of physical proximity
as well."

"In other words, they feel as though someone's
standing or sitting next to them."

"Exactly. Maybe we'll make a parapsychologist out
of you yet."

David smirked, and then asked "So, are we going to
bring Maria in on this one?"

"No, not this time," said Dr. Wayne. "In 44 years this
apparition has never appeared in the immediate presence of a
woman; whatever her motivation may be, it seems both
benign and entirely focused on adult men."

Ladies of the Night

I first wrote this story around 1989, but it was lost when the paper copy vanished and the floppy disc on which it was kept was somehow damaged. I never forgot it, though, and in the winter of 2011 I rewrote it (somewhat better than before, I think). Most of the whores in these tales, whether protagonist or antagonist, are basically on the side of the angels, but this one...well, you'll see.

Spring Forward

Demons are moody, treacherous beings; the spells designed to summon them are full of complex instructions and peculiar requirements, and violation of any of these may break the magical constraints placed upon the entity and allow it to exact a horrible vengeance upon the mortal foolish enough to drag it from its own plane of existence in an attempt to force it into servitude. And given his comparative inexperience at black magic, Howard wasn't about to risk any of the more complicated rituals; he was too squeamish for blood sacrifice, too shaky-handed to inscribe intricate cabalistic diagrams, and too poor at math to trust his calculation of precise astrological conditions, and he wasn't knowledgeable enough to be sure what the various archaic names for certain herbs and powders might actually refer to in modern terminology. But the grimoire he had stolen from an estate he was cataloging for the bank was large and very complete, and his thorough study of it eventually turned up half a dozen spells in which even a novice like himself could feel a reasonable degree of confidence.

He read the descriptions of the specific demons conjured by these more accessible invocations and quickly settled upon the one which appealed most to him: Nahemah, the Princess of Succubae, fallen angel of prostitution and harlot of Hell, who conferred upon he who could command her the gifts of divination and sexual power over any mortal. Considering Howard's meager assets and dismal track record with the opposite sex, this was the demon for him; with divination he could pick winning stocks or horses, and with power over women he could enslave the proud whores who were only interested in him for as long as he could keep paying. He would show them, and other women too; in fact everyone who had ever crossed him would rue the day they had done so once Nahemah was his to command! Best of all, her spell wasn't even difficult; the only critical stipulation was that the final word be pronounced exactly at midnight.

The next day he paid no mind to the lovely spring weather as he drove around town collecting everything he needed for the procedure, and for the rest of the afternoon he devoted himself to laying out his supplies and moving all the furniture to the sides of his living room, then carefully inscribing the protective pentacle on the floor in chalk. He made sure he measured every dimension carefully and precisely copied the arcane words of protection around its rim, then studied the ritual again and practiced pronouncing those Latin words of its text with which he was unfamiliar. He confined his dog in the garage so as to preclude any possibility of her smudging the lines of the diagram and then tested the amount of time it would take him to perform the whole summoning, determining after several trial runs that he should start at 11:30 and pace himself with frequent pauses at junctures where they seemed to be allowed so as to be ready to complete the last phrase as his hall-clock was striking twelve. He then checked that clock and his others against the official time announcement, then prepared a generous supper and after eating allowed himself the rare indulgence of a cigar. "I'll be able to afford these whenever I like once I strike my bargain with Nahemah," he thought, "and a different girl fixing my dinner every night!" His thoughts soon wandered to other pleasures he would enjoy with those women, but he dismissed such fantasies as distracting to his concentration; there would be plenty of time for that later, only it wouldn't be mere fantasy then!

Spring Forward

By 11 PM his nerves were thoroughly frazzled and he had a glass of wine to calm them. He only allowed himself the one; after all this work and preparation he wasn't about to risk his success on slurred speech. In over four decades he had never succeeded at anything worthwhile, and he certainly wasn't going to do anything to risk failure tonight! So he composed himself as best he could, and when he heard the half-hour chime he checked his clocks again, then lit the candles and began the ritual.

Howard's spirits began to rise as he realized that this time he had done everything right; he neither stumbled over the words nor fumbled over the gestures, and the pacing was exactly as he had practiced. Some fifteen minutes into the ceremony his dog began to howl mournfully from the garage; perhaps her keen senses had detected some disturbance in the environment caused by the spell's beginning to work. Then as if in imitation of the dog, the wind outside also began to howl, but he ignored both it and the animal; with his victory so close he could not admit even the slightest distraction. He paused momentarily in his incantation while gesturing and burning a piece of rune-marked parchment, then stole a glance at his watch and began the final phrases of the conjuration, ending just as his clock began to strike twelve.

He did not have long to wait after that; a column of multicolored smoke erupted within the summoning diagram inscribed on the floor and the room was filled with a sweet, complex odor with earthy undertones. Within the vapor a shadowy form appeared, and as the cloud began to dissipate the shape was revealed as that of a hauntingly beautiful woman whose unearthly nature was only betrayed by the fact that her eyes were lightless orbs like two enormous black pearls. The dog's howling was frantic now, and the wind had risen to a gale, and as Nahemah looked upon him with a terrible smile he somehow knew deep in his gut that something was very, very wrong.

"I will never understand mortals," she purred in a voice as sweet as honey and as cold as the void between worlds. "I enjoy coming to your plane so much that I placed as few restrictions on my summoning as possible, yet you blithely ignored my simple requirement and called me hither a full hour before the permitted time. 'Tis a pity; it would have been far more entertaining to trick you into betraying yourself." And with that she stepped forward out of the circle, its power broken by the miscast spell, and her would-be master's scream was abruptly silenced as the two of them vanished like a nightmare on wakening. Poor, incompetent Howard; though he had done his very best to get everything right, it never occurred to him than no mortal government has the power to compel a demon to observe Daylight Saving Time.

Spring Forward

Ladies of the Night

The previous story, as you may have surmised, was in a way written backward; I thought of the "punch line" first, and wrote the story around it (so to speak). In this next one, the climactic scene was literally written first, and then the earlier and later parts.

Ripper

The man walked down the dirty, empty street, keeping to the shadows and avoiding the occasional video camera by carefully plotting his course. There weren't many in this part of town, and those were mostly located at major intersections or near businesses; by travelling in side-streets and alleys he could make it to his hunting ground unobserved. He turned the collar of his overcoat up against the November cold, drew his hat lower on his brow and then returned his hand to his pocket, fingering the surgical knife there. Like the transparent polymer gloves which covered his hands, he had stolen it from the hospital where he worked; fifteen years of experience with institutional procedures allowed him to be certain nobody would ever discover it missing.

The evening damp chilled him to the bone and as the wind bit into him he cursed the activist judges who had tied the hands of the police and released sin and wickedness upon society. In the old days officials knew right from wrong, and the laws allowed police to round up the harlots who tempted men into sin and polluted this once-great nation with their lewdness. But slowly, over time, they had seduced judges and lawmakers, bewitching them into dismantling laws which protected men and their families from wanton women, and now they could brazenly practice their whoredom without fear of punishment. For years he had been sickened by the sight of their advertisements; the adult information channels were befouled by them, and in time he had come to realize that it was the duty of moral and Godly men to perform the task the government had abdicated. He knew it was a sign of weakness in him to complain about the cold

Ladies of the Night

while performing a sacred duty, but surely it wasn't wrong to be angry with the authorities for forcing him out on such an unpleasant night to do their jobs for them.

Unfortunately, the more beautiful and seductive harlots had become wealthy enough by the multitude of their sins to be able to afford bodyguards, and they were so sought-after by lustful men that they could demand thorough screening procedures before seeing them; it was thus impossible for him to reach any of those. Likewise, the pimps and madams who set up brothels hired guards for the whores they employed; he thus had to trust that Divine justice would take care of these pampered and protected hussies. But the degraded trollops who sold their wares on the street, those were within his reach! He had already sent five of the filthy animals to Hell, and God willing he would send another to her well-deserved fate tonight.

As he was about to step from the alley into the street he had chosen for tonight's work, he heard the soft whine of a police cruiser and quickly drew back into the shadows. What irony! They were both on the side of law and righteousness, yet he had to hide from the police because they had been ordered by their corrupt superiors to hunt him down. Oh, yes, they were looking for him, but they wouldn't find him; he was too clever and understood his quarry too well. Though their filthy trade was no longer illegal, streetwalkers rarely bothered to keep their licenses up to date and often violated nuisance laws by approaching men; though they could not be arrested they could certainly be ticketed for these administrative infractions, and since few of them bothered to pay those tickets they were just as interested in avoiding the police as he was. The best areas for hunting them were thus also the safest places, far from the prying eyes of surveillance cameras.

Ripper

He soon found what he was looking for; though the chill of the evening required her to cover her obscene attire with an overcoat her painted face and high heels gave her away. And what honest woman would be on the street alone, especially on a night like this? He boldly walked up to her as she sheltered from the wind in the doorway of a decaying 20th century building and said "Good evening."

Her smile revealed a face that might once have been pretty before it was ruined by indulgence in lusts of the flesh. "Hi," she said in a deceptively sweet voice. "Since it's an awful night to be out, you must be looking for some company."

It disgusted him to have to be social with this creature, but he knew God would forgive him the deception necessary to get her alone where his work would not be disturbed. "Yes, I am. How much?"

"$200," she said. He inwardly recoiled; how could a woman sell herself so cheaply? This foul creature was willing to fornicate with anyone for only a few hours' wages at a real job! But he kept his true feelings from his face and simply nodded. Then she said, "I'm Tina; what's your name?"

"John."

She laughed. "Well, that's OK, Tina ain't my real name either. Come on, let's get out of this weather." With that, she opened the door behind them and led him into the dingy foyer, up a gray concrete staircase which smelled faintly of urine, and down a dismal hall to her room. After closing the door she removed her overcoat, revealing the sort of tacky, sluttish dress he expected.

Ladies of the Night

She then told him to get comfortable; he knew what that meant. Why didn't these whores ever say anything directly? Why did they have to cloak everything in lies and deceit? It just made him that much angrier, and he concentrated on that righteous anger as he removed his overcoat, reaching into his pocket for the knife concealed there.

As he drew it out he tossed the overcoat aside and slammed his body into the whore, bearing her back onto the bed with all his weight; with his left hand choking her to stifle her screams he plunged the surgically-sharp blade into her body just below the left breast. Again and again he drove the knife into her, with most of the blows landing in her abdomen. Blood spattered his clothes, but no matter; his overcoat would cover it on his way home. Like another demon-haunted soul of two centuries past, merely killing these fallen women was not enough for him; he wanted to mutilate them, to tear the flesh from them, to spill their entrails on the floor in order to completely destroy the organs they had so dishonored by their harlotry. But before he could achieve the full release of anger he so badly needed, his knife-hand was abruptly stopped in mid-swing by a viselike grip on his wrist; the pressure was so intense that the knife dropped from suddenly nerveless fingers.

"You have the right to remain silent."

The words were delivered in a quiet, steady soprano completely devoid of emotion, and for a moment he was confused as to their source; but the truth soon dawned on him as the mutilated prostitute *sat up*, his right wrist held immobile in her left hand.

"Anything you say will be recorded as all your words and actions up to now have been, and may be used in evidence in a court of law."

Ripper

It was like a nightmare or some horrible video; the mundane, prescribed words continued to pour calmly and evenly from the mouth of a woman who could not possibly be alive. "You have the right to speak to an attorney. If you cannot afford an attorney, one will be appointed for you. Do you understand these rights as I have explained them to you?"

He nodded dumbly, and she continued. "Please do not struggle; you cannot escape and I have no wish to cause unnecessary injury. I have already called for the police and they will be here within a minute. Do not be afraid; we understand that you are mentally ill and you will be taken to a facility where you can be helped."

As if on cue, a squad of blue-armored policemen filed into the room, accompanied by two men in medical coats. They began to move quietly around the room, taking pictures and collecting samples; one picked up his overcoat, and another lifted his fallen knife with gloved hands and transferred it to a plastic bag. One of the medics examined him, shining a light into his eye while the other injected him with a spray hypodermic. None of them spoke to him, nor he to any of them; after the medic released his head he simply sat there, staring at the mutilated belly of the whore, until a voice said "let's go". Then the woman rose, drawing him up alongside of her, and as she stood a large slab of lacerated muscle fell from her body, revealing beneath a rib of stainless steel.

Ladies of the Night

*The Ouled Nail (pronounced "will-ed nah-eel") were a
Berber tribe who inhabited the Atlas Mountains of Algeria;
though they were converted to Islam in the 7th and 8th
centuries, they kept a number of distinctive characteristics
which set them apart until well into the 20th century. Chief
among these was the status of their women, or* Nailiyat; *not
only were they free from* purdah, *in adolescence they actually
went down into the cities unescorted by men and worked for
a time as dancers and prostitutes in order to amass a
personal fortune with which to purchase property at home,
and only after they had done this would they seek marriage.
The Nailiyat were thus not only remarkably independent by
the standards of tribal cultures or Muslims, but even by the
traditional standards of European cultures; they enjoyed a
freedom unknown by any but the wealthiest, boldest women
before the "sexual revolution", and indeed greater than that
of many "liberated" women to this very day. Their origins
are lost to history, but we can be certain their dancers were
already entertaining travelers by the time the Arabs
appeared. And since the antecedents of the Berbers were
painting on the rocks at Tassili some 2000 years before the
last glaciers retreated from Europe, it may be that their
customs are very ancient indeed and could perhaps be
related to the myth that North Africa was ruled by the
Amazons in the time of Atlantis. I will not ask you to imagine
a period so remote; for the purpose of this story, I ask that
you grant me only that the dancing harlots of Algeria were
already practicing their customs roughly 1000 years before
the advent of the Arabs.*

Dance of the Seasons

"Grandmother, what are they like, the men from the sea? Mother says they are different from our men and even from the nomads and merchants."

"And so they are; they have great wealth and learning, but they are filled with a restlessness which drives them to change the world, so that they are often ill at ease with even their own customs, much less those of others."

The girl's face clearly registered her confusion, so her grandmother said "I shall tell you a story of one such man, a regular patron of mine for many years, and then perhaps you will understand.

"The Wheel of the Year had turned all the way 'round once again, and the sun had come to the place in his dance which signaled it was time for us to go down to the city. And so my husband and brother loaded our camels and we bade them goodbye and rode down to seek our fortunes as I had fourteen times before, and as my mother and her mother before her had ridden in their turns. I was married by that time and so no longer danced or allowed men to come in to my room, but my two younger sisters needed my guidance and that year my own eldest daughter, your mother, was at last old enough to begin working for her own fortune.

"I knew the way well and there were no mishaps, and this well pleased your mother, for she was full of the fire of youth and would have chafed at any delay in her debut. It was all I could do to restrain her enthusiasm sufficiently to enforce rest upon our arrival; given her way she would have been dancing for her first coins ere the sun set! But the next day was soon enough; as I told her there was no need for

Ladies of the Night

haste, and she would not be any the poorer at season's end
for having rested from her journey.

"The next night we laughed, her aunts and I, as I had
known we would; all the years of lessons could not have
prepared her for the exhaustion of body and mind one feels
after one's first day of dancing for strangers. But she had
done well, and the men had been kind, and I knew that by the
time the merchants from Carthage started to appear in a few
weeks she would be ready to impress them as I had done at
her age. And this was important, as it will be for you, for in
addition to their gold they bring pearls, incense, perfumes,
raisin wine and fine purple cloth, and other precious things
from across the sea. But to gain these treasures one must
employ all of her charms to stand out from the other girls, for
Carthage is a great city and her men have seen wonders and
lain with the beauties of many nations.

"Soon they came as they always did, few in number
but with sufficient guards to protect the expensive goods they
brought to our land to trade; they were met by nomads
bringing gold, ivory and precious stones and sometimes even
the elephants the Carthaginians prize for their army. And
when the trading was done for the day they wanted
entertainment, and I am proud to say your mother won their
money with as much skill as some girls who had been
dancing for years. I knew that they were led by a man who
was very fond of me, Mago by name, because he had already
sent one of his servants to ask if he might visit me that
evening as had been his custom for fourteen years."

"But surely you did not lie with him!"

"No, child; when I found a husband I gave up earning
money thus, as you will when your turn comes. But he still
enjoyed dining with me and talking to me, and as the needs
of his body could be satisfied by my younger sisters he was

Dance of the Seasons

content to respect my vows. But I found my old friend in a strange humor that evening; he was strangely silent at dinner, and ate little of the fine food I had prepared for him. He seemed overwhelmed with melancholy, and asked me strange questions he had never asked before; 'Why do you live in this way?' he asked, and 'Do you not want better for your daughter?' It quickly became clear to me that it was the presence of your mother which had affected him so; he knew of our customs, and indeed had met my own mother in the days when she travelled to town with me. But because he had come to know me, it seemed to him a different thing for me to train my own daughter as a harlot than for others to do so.

"'This is the way of our people,' I told him, 'and it has ever been so since the days when antelope grazed on the grasses of this land which is now a desert. I learned the craft from my mother, as she learned from hers, and so on back to the Great Mothers of the beginning. And as I have taught my daughter so she shall teach hers, and each shall dance and work and love in her season until the end of the world.' But my words only agitated him; he spoke of 'progress', and 'sacrifice', and the latter word came with great bitterness and eyes shining with unshed tears. I told him I did not understand, and he said that it was our job to build a better world for our children, one which was kinder to them; I replied, 'any changes we make to the world are mortal, just as the things of the world itself. Did you not yourself tell me long years ago that Carthage is the daughter of an older empire, now since fallen into ruin? And no doubt that empire was built on the bones of another, and one day great Carthage herself must die as we all die. Each learns from those that

Ladies of the Night

have come before, as we learn our trade from our mothers; each dances in her youth, and accumulates wealth and stature, and brings forth offspring and then moves on. Summer gives way to autumn, and autumn to winter; we can teach and advise the young, but they must earn their own rewards. We cannot do it for them, nor force them to live in a way appropriate to the mature or old.'

"But it was no use; he heard my words but there was a secret pain in him, something of which he would not speak, and he looked upon your mother and sighed with profound sadness. Then he took from his satchel a great treasure, a jar of the purple dye worth twenty times its weight in gold, and presented it to me in trust for your mother, 'To hasten the day when she can buy a house and have daughters of her own,' he said. Then he embraced us both and left, and never again did I see him after that night, though she and I returned every season, always staying in the same house, until she married."

Dihya sat quietly for a moment, and then shook her head and said, "Strange indeed." And then, "Thank you, grandmother," and excused herself to join a group of her friends she had espied through the window.

Her mother had remained quiet throughout the story, but after the girl had quit the room she spoke. "Though almost twenty years have passed I well remember that night, and often have I thought upon the man who endowed me with such a valuable gift, yet asked for nothing in return. Was it merely a token of his love for you?"

"No, it was more than that," the older woman said. "He and I were both reasonably certain that he was your father."

Dance of the Seasons

Ladies of the Night

As mentioned earlier, my stories usually contain clues to alert readers to the time setting, but I was unusually careful with this one; a clever reader (with internet access for some minor research) will be able to determine the exact date on which this story takes place. Bonus points if you can name the movie they're going to see.

Ambition

One may be old in years, but not in spirit, or poor in wealth, but not in ambition. - Chinese proverb

Though Rosemary wouldn't have admitted it, she was *very* relieved to have a date for that night. It wasn't that she doubted her plan; she was an intelligent and resourceful girl and realized that, though it might seem counterintuitive, one of the surest ways to succeed as a call girl was to pretend one already had plenty of money. So she had left the brothel at which she was formerly employed, invested in a new wardrobe, taken a small but fashionable apartment with her sister as housekeeper and secretary, and even had a private telephone installed. She then let her regulars know she was out on her own, took out personals ads in the papers and waited for the results.

In these black times, it was an incredibly bold move; but as her Grandmother O'Malley had always said, the only thing she had more of than spunk was luck. And though some of her friends thought she was crazy, Colleen had faith in her and the two of them kept each others' spirits up for months as her assets dwindled and her new clientele failed to materialize. Oh, they weren't in danger of starving; Rosemary had some good regulars and always made the rent on time, though it often took spending more time in bars than she would have liked. But unless she started attracting the kind of gents she was aiming for, sooner or later she would become financially unable to project the high-class illusion on which her image depended.

She also felt ashamed of being unable to buy her sister the same sort of nice things she bought for herself. Of

Ladies of the Night

course, every time the subject came up Colleen just pooh-poohed her concern and pointed out that it wasn't important because the gentlemen never saw *her*, and that she was lucky to have such a generous sister now that jobs were so hard to come by. That was the sort of girl Colleen was; loyal and uncomplaining, as their mother had been…and it just made Rosemary feel worse. So much worse, in fact, that she had spent entirely too much money on Christmas presents for her. And after that, and filling the icebox with food for their Christmas dinner, there wasn't exactly a lot left in her bank account; the call had therefore been a godsend.

Luckily, this had been the warmest autumn Rosemary could remember, so their heating costs had been almost nonexistent; the mild weather also made it possible for her to save cab fare tonight by walking to the client's place, which was only eight blocks away. She hesitated a bit upon seeing the building; though it was certainly no tenement, it also didn't look like the sort of place in which a man who could afford to blow $20 for an hour with a good-time girl might live. But she trusted her luck and her instincts, and the latter told her to go inside.

She was admitted to a well-kept apartment by a young man who, despite his mature demeanor and clothing, couldn't have been a day over 17. This was unexpected; Rosemary had sometimes been received by valets or maids, but never a client's son! Still, times being what they were, she subdued her expression of surprise. "Hi, kiddo! Where's your dad?"

"He died in the war when I was just a baby."

"Gee, I'm sorry! Your older brother, then."

"I'm an only child; it's just me and Ma here." At the mention of a woman Rosemary started to retreat with a mumbled apology, but the young man stopped her with, "Oh, she's not here, she cleans an office building at night."

Ambition

"Look, I'm sorry, I must have the wrong address."

"Aren't you Rosemary?"

"Yeah, but who are you?"

"I'm Bill." It was the name the client had given. He certainly hadn't sounded as young on the telephone as he looked in person.

"Wow, Bill…look, I'm sorry but…aren't you too young to be engaging in this sort of pastime?"

With an air of seriousness which belied his age, he asked, "What difference does that make if I can pay?"

"No offense but…$20 is more money than most guys your age can afford."

He was unperturbed. "I left school two years ago to help Ma out; the man who owns the radio shop down the street hired me and taught me to repair them. He says I'm a natural. One day I want to have a shop of my own, so I've been saving up."

"A smart, good-looking young guy like you probably has every girl in the neighborhood after him!"

"Yeah, but I can't stand girls my age; they're too silly. Not a one of them has the brains to talk about the sort of things I'm interested in."

Rosemary had already noticed the stack of *Amazing Stories*, *Weird Tales* and other magazines of fantasy and scientifiction. "What makes you think I'm not just as silly as they are?"

"Because my boss told me about you."

"He *what*?"

"Don't get angry; he knows I'm trustworthy and tells me things he wouldn't tell his own brother. And besides, he was drunk at the time. He sees you often and he really likes you."

Rosemary now knew who the boss was, and what sorts of things he had probably said. "Bill, you understand that this isn't like a regular date, right? I mean, I charge by the hour."

He looked a bit sheepish. "Well, I was sort of hoping that once I hired you a few times, you might get to like me and maybe we could just go out together sometimes. Like as friends, I mean I wouldn't expect the other stuff. Just like movies or dinner or..." he trailed off.

In spite of her annoyance, she had to admire his moxie. In a way, they were kindred spirits; both were unconventional dreamers with a yen to succeed on their own terms and the drive to make it happen. After a short pause, she said, "Well, what are you waiting for?"

"Excuse me?"

"Get your hat and coat. You called me for a date, remember? And if we're going to get good seats for that new Boris Karloff movie, we'd better step on it."

His face broke into a huge grin, and he hustled to get his clothes, then suddenly stopped with a crestfallen look. "I can't afford two hours."

"Keep the money, except for cab fare and the cost of my ticket and my popcorn. Save it for that radio shop, or get your Ma a new coat for Christmas. I can always use another friend, and besides I've been thinking of buying a radio, and maybe you can help me pick one."

The grin returned, and in seconds they were out the door and on their way toward the future.

Ambition

Ladies of the Night

On the second day of my blog, a friend of mine commented that he'd like to see a prostitute as adventure heroine. The idea appealed to me so much that I was inspired to write this story a week later; I've managed to turn out one per month without fail since then. So though this wasn't my first story with a hooker character, it was the first one written with that particular point in mind.

The Trick

"Almost ready?" asked Van, sticking his head into the bathroom where Bella was checking her makeup.

"Just about," she replied, "I had to make sure I had enough supplies in my purse."

"So, what do you think?" he asked.

"Not sure. He sounded promising."

Van nodded. "Well, the car's ready when you are. Where are we going?"

"The Downtown Hilton," she said, picking up her purse and gesturing him to move back from the doorway. "Let's go."

She relaxed and collected herself while Van drove her to the hotel; it made her job so much easier to know that she had a partner in whom she could completely rely. His mere presence was reassuring, and he had never failed to be exactly where she needed him to be exactly when she needed it; having him as a partner made an impossible job merely difficult. As if he could hear her thoughts, he reached over and gently patted her leg, giving her thigh a reassuring squeeze.

They soon arrived at the hotel, and she gave him a quick peck on the cheek before getting out. The autumn night had turned unexpectedly chilly, and she clutched her filmy shawl a little more tightly about her shoulders as she hastened into the big revolving door. In a few moments she was through, and with practiced nonchalance walked over to the bank of elevators and chose an empty car in which to ascend to the 23rd floor. She consulted her notebook to be sure of the room number, checked her face and hair in the elevator's mirror and stepped out into the quiet hall as soon as the doors opened. The numbering system in this hotel was pretty straightforward, and before long she found the room and knocked on the door.

When she had first started this job three months ago, the interval between her knocking and the answer seemed interminable; she had always felt exposed and obvious in the hall for an impossible length of time before the door was opened and she could begin the process of feeling the individual customer out. But within a week her confidence had increased, and now it always seemed as though the client was literally waiting at the door; this time was no exception.

"Byron," as he had called himself on the phone, was a striking man, proverbially tall, dark and handsome and endowed with a magnetism Bella could almost feel. She remembered how she used to believe that all of a hooker's clients were fat, old, ugly or otherwise unable to pick up women, but it had not taken her long to discover how mistaken that notion was; in her experience there were just as many attractive men among her clientele as in the general population. In any case, it was neither here nor there; she had a job to do, and had schooled herself to be immune to the charms of those with whom she did it. So she smiled her prettiest smile, introduced herself, and stepped into the room.

While he closed the hall door, she walked down the narrow little hall past the closed bathroom door and made a quick appraisal of the room; she was struck by its sheer messiness. Not filth, mind; there were no pizza boxes or beer cans or overflowing garbage or any of the other typical rubbish one sometimes encountered in clients' rooms. No, this was just clutter, a sheer volume of luggage and clothes which told her that Byron could not have come by air unless he owned the plane. Several large suitcases stood in the space between the bed and the curtained window, while garment bags and loose clothing draped every available hook and fixture. "Goodness,

The Trick

what a mess!" Bella exclaimed; she had discovered that plain honest conversation usually made a better impression than pretense or flattery.

Byron laughed. "Sorry about this," he said; "I'm going to be in town for a while and I like to be comfortable. Please don't be put off by it."

"Not at all," said Bella with a smile, but inside she was keyed up; she had noticed a telling detail, and knew that she must be on her guard at all costs. But he hadn't done anything really unusual yet, and she had to be absolutely sure. So she continued with, "I like to get the formalities out of the way first, so I can check in with the agency and then we can relax." As he pulled out his wallet, he reminded her that she had agreed to stay the full hour, and she nodded and assured him that she always took as much time with her customers as was needed.

He handed over the cash, and she thanked him sweetly and put it into her purse, then picked up the phone to call the agency. After noting the time and checking in, she turned again to Byron and said "So, what did you have in mind tonight?"

"Oh, I just thought we'd chat for a few minutes first; there's no need to rush things," he said. "How long have you been doing this?"

"I'm pretty new at it," she said, "only three months now." She had discovered that an honest response to that question generally got a good reaction, and this time was no exception.

"Three months! Why, that practically makes you a *virgin*!" This was said with a sort of condescending undertone that Bella did not at all like, but she was here to do

Ladies of the Night

her job and so pretended to laugh at his "joke". He continued, "Aren't you ever scared?"

This wasn't an unusual question, but the mockery in his voice drove her to a higher state of alarm which she nevertheless kept from her face. "Sure, sometimes," she said. "But the agency knows exactly where I am, so if I don't call out on time they can call my driver downstairs."

As she expected, he was unfazed. "That didn't help those other girls, though. How many now, eight in the past few months?"

"Nine," she answered, unable to keep the choke out of her voice. The sick bastard was enjoying this; he wanted to terrify her before having his way with her, but she fought down the fear and continued to watch him with poorly-feigned nonchalance.

"Haven't the police any leads?" he continued, attempting to meet her gaze.

She turned the slightly to the right and squeaked, "No, none of the bodies have been found, and he keeps changing hotels. And besides, the cops never try very hard when it's whores who are vanishing." Then, abruptly, "Look, do we really need to talk about this? Wouldn't you prefer to do what you hired me for?"

Then he laughed, and in an instant Bella erupted into action. In one smooth motion she drew the pistol from her purse and swept the obscuring clothing from the bureau mirror, ascertaining in an instant that she was the only person reflected in it before turning to fire three perfect shots straight into the rapidly-approaching Byron's heart. He clutched his chest with a look of complete astonishment, then collapsed onto the floor at her feet.

She did not hesitate for a moment, but put three more shots into his back, confident that the sharp "Thwip! Thwip!

The Trick

Thwip!" of the silenced weapon would not be audible in the next room above the sound of the television set. Her hands shaking, she dropped again into the chair and called Van. "It's done," she sighed.

"So it *was* him! I'll be right up!" While she waited, she opened the largest of the suitcases; as she expected, it was empty but for bloodstains. She showed Van when he arrived, and with carefully-controlled anger he said "This time it's *his* turn to be carried out in it." Then he unshouldered his bag and she turned away; no matter how many times they did this, she would never be able to watch Van decapitate them. She knew that Byron had been dead for a long time, decades maybe, and that he was no longer human but a hellish monster who preyed on unsuspecting women. But try as she might she just couldn't handle the sight or sound of the head coming off, and Van understood; as usual, he waited until she left the room.

She felt stronger as she walked out into the cold night air and went to the car to wait for Van to arrive with the loaded suitcase; as usual, they would torch its contents on their way out of town. As she waited, looking up at the moon, she felt her face creep into a smile; she was going to miss being a call girl. Her cover for this mission had been a lot more interesting than posing as a coed, a barfly or any of the other kinds of women their quarries usually preyed on, and it had been even more lucrative than the time she had played the part of a stripper. One thing was for certain; the money she had made in the past few months would not only support them for quite a while between hunts, but also purchase quite a number of silver bullets.

Ladies of the Night

*Every author will tell you that inspiration can come from all
sorts of places. This story was written only two weeks after "A
Decent Boldness", and sprung almost fully formed from a
conversation I had with my husband while driving him to the
airport. I hope you enjoy it, though you may find it a bit...
disquieting.*

Concubine

It had been a few weeks since the new Chief had moved in, but Desiree (the oldest member of the Harem, who had been there through two previous changes of power) said that it usually took at least that long for them to get settled in, familiarize themselves with the myriad administrative responsibilities of the position and have enough free time to sample the spoils of victory. Olga, the youngest of the women, had finally stopped crying (she had become genuinely fond of the last Master of the House) and resigned herself to her duties, and the others constantly gossiped about the man with whom they would all become intimately acquainted in the next few months. But Fatima, as usual, was pragmatic about the whole thing; in her mind one man was much like another. They had a job to do and there wasn't much point in their whining about their situation or wondering what other kinds of lives they might've had if things had been different. Every woman here had been given a choice; each had chosen to become a Concubine in order to save her family from ruin, and each had vanished from the world of sunlight and freedom into the gilded cage of the Harem.

Viewed dispassionately, it wasn't a bad life at all; they were treated to the best of everything, could do virtually anything they liked which didn't involve going out in public, had servants to prepare their meals and keep their quarters clean, and only had to work once a week at most; those who were less favored for one reason or another might only work once a month. And their pay was more than most of them could have earned on the outside; Fatima and Desiree made

Ladies of the Night

much less than they had as free harlots, but being relieved of the need to find new customers and the constant threat of police persecution made up for it.

The memories leapt unbidden into Fatima's mind; four years ago she had been hunted down and trapped, and then a man had come to her cell to make her the offer. Given that the alternative was relentless and lifelong pursuit of every person she had ever cared about on false charges supported by paid informants and fabricated evidence, how could she refuse? She felt the anger rising and fought it down. *It doesn't matter*, she thought; *the world isn't fair.* Many women are raped, or end up with abusive husbands, or work themselves into early graves with drudgery, or develop terminal diseases and die in long-protracted agony; her life was pleasant and she was protected from all harm. The only thing missing was freedom, and was she any less free than a woman with five children to support? Freedom is largely an illusion anyway.

She decided that the best thing would be to simply immerse herself in preparations; she had been notified earlier that her services would be required this evening, and though the scheduled time wasn't for hours yet she wanted to make a good first impression, and that required composing herself so her face would reveal no trace of disquiet. She had no desire to offend this one as poor Ruth had offended his predecessor; after their first time together, he had only ever called her when he felt in a particularly sadistic mood. No, far better to be sweet, accommodating and enthusiastic than to risk living like that until another rival took his place years from now. So she took a long, hot bath, burned her favorite incense while meditating, took her time selecting a flattering outfit and then carefully applied her makeup before calling in the

Concubine

hairdresser, a chubby little lady with a maternal manner who could always make her smile.

Eventually it was almost time, and she went out into the common area where all of the other Concubines were waiting to hug and kiss her and wish her good luck. Olga started crying again and Fatima reassured her that it would be all right, then told all of them that she would share her experience when she returned so they would have some idea of what to expect when their turns came. The guard was waiting to escort her when she stepped outside the door, and together they travelled along carpeted corridors until they reached the elevator, in which she rode up alone. Her heart was pounding as it had when she was about to meet her very first client almost a decade ago, but she took slow, deep breaths to calm herself and when the elevator doors opened she glided gracefully forward into the presence of the most powerful man in the world. Dropping a deep curtsy, she greeted him:

"Good evening, Mr. President; I'm very pleased to meet you."

Ladies of the Night

*Though most of my science fiction futures are of the
optimistic variety, the dystopian setting is a way for a writer
to issue a warning without coming across as overly priggish
or paranoid. I fervently hope that things do not continue in
the direction that will soon take us to this near-future
nightmare, but...*

Fair Game

The terrorist and the policeman both come from the same basket. Revolution, legality–counter-moves in the same game; forms of idleness at bottom identical.
- Joseph Conrad

"You've done quite well the past few years, Simon," said Andrew, looking around the apartment at the expensive furnishings. "Honestly, I've always agreed with Dad; I never thought you'd amount to much."

"Thanks for the vote of confidence."

"I'm only trying to say that I was wrong. Not everyone's good at study, very few have what it takes to succeed at politics, and none of our family has a head for business. But you've really managed to capitalize on these new laws."

Though he lacked Andrew's intellectual brilliance, Simon was by no means stupid when it came to people; he knew his older brother was sneering at him. "We can't all be college professors."

"No, that's true. And though you started much later, it looks like you've passed me in the income department. But aren't you afraid of getting caught?"

"What do you mean, 'caught'?"

"Well, bounty hunting is technically illegal; a felony, in fact. And that means you're just as vulnerable under the Citizen's Law Enforcement Act as anybody."

"Not really; they have to tolerate it or the whole system falls apart. You know as well as I do why they passed CLEA: crime rates were skyrocketing while revenues were tanking, and all the available police manpower is tied

81

up suppressing riots and fighting the big crime gangs. Polls show it's a very popular program; the bounties cost far less than police salaries and benefits, and they're more than covered by the seized assets of captured criminals."

"Some people call those riots 'protests', and point out that the crime rates wouldn't be soaring if the government didn't keep inventing new crimes. Some even say that the program is nothing more than a way to rob the citizenry under color of law."

"Whatever. You and I both know that's not going to change anytime soon, and I'm going to get mine while I can. As you pointed out, I haven't exactly succeeded at any other kind of work."

"No, you haven't." Simon thought for a moment he was going to say something else, but apparently he thought better of it and kept his mouth shut for a change. The conversation turned to the wars in Nigeria and Venezuela, the upcoming Super Bowl and their mother's health, and after he left Simon got himself a snack and looked over the evening's plans on his phone. He then showered, shaved and dressed and headed out for his appointment.

He was really looking forward to this one; it had involved considerable research, and as Andrew would happily point out that wasn't his strong suit. But it looked like the tip would prove worth the money he had paid for it; there was a high bounty on sex traffickers, and his cut of her assets would be worth much more than that. Best of all, he would be able to get the kind of sex he liked best before bringing her in, with no chance of getting in trouble for it.

As arranged, he met "Regina" at an exclusive restaurant and he immediately paid her by bumping phones. The fee was high and the dinner would be as well, but one had to be willing to spend money up front to succeed in this

Fair Game

business. For instance, he could never have passed her screening without the pricey undercover alias service to which he paid out four figures a month, nor could he have been reasonably sure she was the woman he was after without expensive software to crack the distortion all escorts now used to protect against facial recognition programs. And the miniature DNA analyzer was vital for ensuring he didn't open himself up to a ruinous lawsuit by bringing in the wrong person.

But none of this would be worth a damn without the natural skills his pompous ass of a brother could never recognize as such: the hunter's instinct that helped him track his quarry, and the gambler's poker face that now allowed him to chat charmingly with a beautiful woman without giving as much as a hint of a sign that he was planning to rape her, abduct her and turn her over to the police for years of prison followed by a lifetime of Registration.

Everything so far had gone according to plan, and when she went to the ladies' room after dinner he took the opportunity to activate the app which interfaced with the DNA analyzer; it was a positive match. Her surprisingly-flattering mug shot came up on the screen, along with her real name and criminal record: Dorothy Jenkins, born September 29, 1988; convictions for pandering, money laundering and conspiracy. That gave him his threshold; she was fair game.

They returned to her incall, where he was pleased to see that she trusted her screening methods; there was neither bodyguard nor maid, which would make his job even easier. They relaxed for a while, had drinks on the sofa, continued the conversation, and then when the time seemed right

Ladies of the Night

headed for the bedroom. She undressed him, caressed him, and massaged his back with a fragrant oil; she then slid off the bed, removed her earrings and did something on her nightstand…and suddenly Simon felt searing pain tear through his entire being. He tried to scream, but couldn't; every muscle in his body seemed frozen in place. The pain came again, and once more, and then through blurry, watering eyes he saw her bending over him, reading from the screen of her phone. And he heard her voice as though it were at the far end of a tube:

"Simon Bailey, born April 18th, 1985; convictions for assault on a police officer and illegal gambling; suspected of 67 counts of human trafficking for the purpose of exploitation of the Citizen's Law Enforcement Act. Bounty hunting's a felony, smart guy, and that makes you fair game."

Fair Game

Ladies of the Night

Not everyone with supernatural abilities wants to get rich, fight crime or take over the world; some just want to meet interesting people.

Bucket List

**Striving toward a goal puts a more pleasing construction
on our advance toward death.** - Mason Cooley

Anthony trudged down the filthy street, pulling his
cloak down as far as he could to keep out the evening rain.
Anyone who observed his erratic course would have thought
him drunk, but every sane Roman was out of the beastly
weather and Anthony's weaving route was shaped by the
necessity of avoiding puddles while yet getting close enough
to the signs to read them in the darkness without having to
uncover his head.

He had occupied himself thus every night for most of
a week, making inquiries and crossing palms with *sestertii* in
an effort to discover the location of his quarry, and he was
beginning to despair; he felt as though he had walked every
muddy, narrow, winding back-street in the city, and the foul
weather had dampened his spirits as thoroughly as it had his
clothes. His schoolboy Latin was insufficient to the task at
hand, and his outlandish accent and incredible ignorance of
mundane matters marked him as a barbarian at best and a
madman at worst; he feared that small-time hucksters were
now pointing him out to one another as one who could be
taken for a few coins merely by pretending to know of the
strumpet he sought so assiduously. If he spent much more he
would be unable to pay her fee, however nominal it might be;
he therefore resolved that if he could not find her by the end
of the night (or maybe sooner than that), he would simply
pass her by, move on to the next name on his list and return
here after he had done enough research to limit his
possibilities to a few easily-investigated locales.

Ladies of the Night

The very worst disappointment was the sheer number
of bad leads; in any era the stage-names of whores tended to
be predictable and repetitive, and some girls were willing to
pretend to be the one for whom he was looking. But so far,
none of the six Lyciscas he had met had been the right one;
each had been too old, too young, too thin, too ugly or too
dark to be *the* Lycisca he wanted to hire. So tonight, he
would follow a different strategy; he would simply go into
each *lupanar* he found, quiz the *villicus* about the women
available that night, and then ask the name of any who fit the
correct description rather than supplying them with the
means of deceiving him in order to deplete his rapidly-
diminishing funds still further.

But just when he was ready to give up, Fortuna
smiled upon him. The streets and the buildings had all begun
to look alike, so he was not surprised when the cashier at one
of the brothels greeted him as a returning customer; he was
about to turn to go when he realized he had been asked a
question in which the name "Lycisca" had been embedded.

"What you saying?" Anthony asked, realizing the
grammatical error as soon as the words were out of his
mouth.

"I said, aren't you the fellow who was looking for
Lycisca a few days ago?"

"Yes," he replied wearily, expecting another con.

"Well, she's here tonight. She wasn't last time you
came, so I tried to give you another girl," he said with a grin.
"But I promise, this is really the Lycisca you're looking for.
Here, I'll call her out where you can see her in the light."

Anthony guessed that the willingness of the *villicus* to
make this extra effort was due to the poor traffic on such a
foul night, but he just couldn't get his hopes up…and then he
saw her. The quality of her blonde wig was out of place in

such a cheap establishment, and the quality of her health out of place in a low-end Roman prostitute. Despite her imposture of a common whore he could see the *hauteur* and breeding in her manner, and the difference between her Latin and that of the plebeians with whom he had been dealing for the past few days was obvious even to his foreign ears. He quickly paid her fee and tipped the cashier extra for remembering him, returned with her to her grimy little room and eagerly did what he had come so far and worked so hard to do.

He awakened to firm but gentle shaking, and opened his eyes to the smiling face of Leon, the one orderly he genuinely liked.

"Good morning, Professor! I'm sorry to disturb you, but I know you don't want to miss breakfast!"

"Good morning, Leon. And thank you for waking me."

"Did you scratch another name off of your list last night?" Then in response to the older man's puzzled expression, "It's the only time you oversleep."

"How well you know me! Yes, I've just returned from a tryst with Valeria Messalina, Empress of Rome."

"How'd you get an empress to sleep with you? I thought you just saw hookers?"

"Messalina was, as you young people say, 'kinky'. She liked to sneak out of the palace while her husband was asleep and work as a common prostitute."

"Wow, is that so? How was she?"

He considered for a moment, cleaning his glasses before putting them on. "Neither as talented as Nell Gwyn nor as beautiful as La Belle Otero, but she made up for that with her sheer exuberance."

"Gee, Professor, I sure wish I could learn that astro-whatsis…"

"Astral projection."

"…astral projection," he repeated, "so I could visit all those historical places like you do."

"Well, Leon, it takes years of study and practice, but I'm sure you could learn if you set your mind to it."

"Naw," he said sheepishly, helping Anthony with his bathrobe, "I'm just big and dumb, I was never good at studies. Who's the next lady you plan to see?"

"I think I shall brush up on my Greek," he said wistfully; "I seem to have a yen for empresses these days."

Bucket List

Ladies of the Night

The lady to whom the Professor was alluding at the end of the previous story is Theodora (500-548), a courtesan who rose to become empress of the Byzantine Empire and later, a Greek Orthodox saint. Her life is already pretty amazing without having to imagine her as being visited by a time traveler, but that's the fun of speculative fiction involving real historical figures or famous literary characters. For example, do you ever speculate on what might have happened next if the events of one of your favorite stories or movies had gone just a little differently? I know I do.

Mercy

Thou art no longer lonely in the world.
- Nathaniel Hawthorne

I sometimes feel sorry for those who don't have a calling. In the course of my life, I meet so many people whose jobs are nothing more than a way to earn a living; not a source of satisfaction or meaning, nor a sacred duty or trust, nor a labor of love, but rather just a means of keeping body and soul together. Now, that's not so bad for young men who are working their way through school, or young women who are just marking time until the right man comes along. But for the poor women forced to lead lives of drudgery, or the men whose sacred fire has been quenched by years at a dead-end job, it must be horrible.

That's why I'm so very thankful to be one of those who feel *called* to my work; as a young girl in Padua I was well-educated but quite sheltered, and since my dear father left me with more than enough to support me in great comfort I was quite content to while away the years in the study of medicine, philosophy and literature, and to amuse myself puttering in the garden. And so things might have remained had not Fortune declared otherwise; with the collapse of my country's economy after the last war I was ruined, and so I took what remained and, like so many of my countrymen, came here to the New World to start a new life.

Though I probably know more of the secrets of the healing arts than all but the most gifted physicians, my learning was drawn entirely from my father's tutelage and my own extensive studies after his death; I had no diploma from a university to set before the eyes of the stolid old men

93

who ran the hospitals, nor could they be bothered to administer to a woman (let alone one for whom English was not her mother tongue) the practical and oral examinations by which I could have proved my skill. But while my sex and heavy accent presented barriers to my gaining employment as a doctor, they also provided me with the tools necessary to charm my way into a position as a nurse. And this proved a blessing in disguise, for it was through that situation that I eventually awakened to my true vocation.

The hospital at which I worked was recognized as a leader in caring for those who had been mutilated by traumatic injuries, both in their immediate care and in the complications that might arise in the months and years to come. It was soon recognized that I showed not the slightest revulsion or faintness in dealing with even the most horrifying disfigurement, and so naturally I was always assigned to deal with such cases. I firmly believe that they err who treat all maladies as merely things of the body, and that the spiritual component cannot be neglected; accordingly, I spent as much time as possible conversing with my patients, giving them encouragement in order to prevent their sinking into despair due to the great misfortunes which had come upon them. My long-term patients and those with chronic complaints soon came to rely upon me to lift their spirits, and would often share their troubles to me.

I had been working there some two years when I had the conversation which changed my life, with a young man who had left most of his lower body behind when he was brought home from the Argonne. The consequences of his injuries were severe, recurrent and worsening, and the prognosis was that he had not long to live. He often spoke to me of his troubles, and one quiet night when the ward was otherwise empty we were able to have a long and intimate

Mercy

conversation, because there was no one else I had to attend to; it was then he confided the source of his greatest pain to me.

"It's not the dyin' part," he said; "'cause I knew when I went 'over there' that there was a chance of that, an' livin' as half a man ain't really livin' anyhow. It's just that – an' I'm sorry to be so blunt, Bea, but I don't know how else to say it – well, I sure wish I could've enjoyed a lady before I went."

Then and there, I knew what I had to do. I had never kissed a man before, but I had seen enough of it in the cinema to know how it was done; moreover, I was fully aware of the effect it would have. I stole a glance to be absolutely sure we were alone, and then I gave him as long and passionate a kiss as I dared. A look of wonderment crossed his face, and I whispered a promise in his ear and told him I would return later. He passed peacefully sometime before morning, with a serene and contented smile on his face.

At first, I found all of my gentlemen in a similar fashion, and arranged to meet them at their homes when I was off duty. But after a time I realized that it was not only the maimed who needed me, but others as well – the chronically ill, the very old, the hopelessly alienated, the desperately lonely – all of them could benefit from my ministrations. And as I grew more worldly I recognized that I could make a far more comfortable living at my new calling than I ever could as a nurse; furthermore, there were men in want of my help all over this great country, so I could hardly afford to be tied to any one place. As the years went by I got very good at seeking them out, at determining which of them

Ladies of the Night

really needed me and which I should pass by, at securing payment in advance, and at avoiding those who could not accept my profession and would surely have harassed or even imprisoned me had they recognized what I was doing.

Now the world is embroiled in another great war, and some say America will soon enter it as well; if that does happen, I will be ready to give peace to its victims. My father, Heaven forgive him, employed his esoteric skill to "protect" me from men by making it impossible for any living thing to survive contact with my flesh; the process thus rendered me immune to disease and decay, and I look today much as I have for well over a century. Through decades of experiment I succeeded in rendering casual contact harmless, yet I am still poisonous to the core; any man with whom I am intimate will within hours fall gently and painlessly into the sleep from which there is no awakening. So though normal relationships and children are forever forbidden to me, I have at last found a vital role in the world as the handmaiden of Death, calling him to those for whom his presence is not dread, but welcome.

(*With grateful acknowledgement to Nathaniel Hawthorne*).

Mercy

Ladies of the Night

You'll see a few more of those acknowledgments to authors who helped to inspire stories in this collection, but in all the other cases ("Palindrome", "Pearls Before Swine" and "Visions of Sugarplums") the inspiration is much less direct; their themes are similar to those of stories written by the authors acknowledged in postscript as Hawthorne was here, and I wished to credit any possible unconscious inspiration. This next one isn't one of them, but it is one of my personal favorites.

Bad News

The eternal Venus…is one of the seductive forms of the Devil. - Charles Baudelaire

"It's settled then; Xoblah will tell Her."

"No, it is *not* settled! Why does it always have to be *me* who brings Her bad news? She's started to call me 'Petrel' because She says my arrival always presages a storm."

"But, sweetie, that's just it; when *you* bring Her bad news She just calls you names, but whenever anyone *else* does it she's set upon by dozens of cats, or thrown out of Heaven, or some other horrible thing. Remember the time She turned Ardath into an incubus?"

All eyes turned to the named girl, who softly moaned "It was *awful*!"

Xoblah sighed; "All right, all right." She hesitated for a moment and then asked, "What name is She using these days?" The others looked askance, coughed or pretended not to hear the question. "Well?"

Empusa (who seemed to have been elected spokeswoman) answered in a low voice, "Ishtar."

"*What*? You want me to bring Her bad news while She's using *Ishtar*? She only goes by that name when She's in an especially belligerent mood! Can't this wait for a few years until She starts using 'Venus' or 'Astarte' again?"

Empusa gave her a pained look. "The longer we wait, the worse it will be."

Xoblah knew she was right; the goddess hated being kept in the dark, and if She found out that the succubae had failed to tell Her about this problem in a timely fashion,

99

they'd be lucky if She didn't hurl them all into Tarterus for a few decades. Still, she needed time to build up her courage before facing the inevitable. "Why must mortals be so difficult?" she asked, to nobody in particular. "Why must they *complicate* everything? Out of the goodness of Her heart, the Love Goddess Herself recruited us, gave us eternal beauty, and empowered us to give the gift of sexual bliss to worthy mortals who weren't getting any for whatever reason. And at first it was *such* an easy job!"

The others nodded in agreement. Habondia observed, "We never *really* had any problems at all until the Middle Ages."

"Even that wasn't so bad," said Empusa, "once we learned to stay away from the Christian priests. It wasn't until they somehow managed to convince themselves that sex was bad for them that it got really difficult."

"But it really looked like things were improving again after the Seventeenth Century," said Xoblah. "And the past few decades were as good as any; wasn't it a laugh when we would appear as mortal women, and then the men would send their experiences with us to be published in magazines and everyone assumed they were making it up?"

"Those sure were fun times," sighed Relah. "But now it seems like they're all afraid of us again. The other day one insisted I provide him with an identification card, then kept asking me silly questions to prove my age."

"Wait until you get one who wants to know where the hidden camera is," said Empusa gloomily. "Or one who just wants to sit and watch porn with you."

"The ones who insist on asking permission for everything are the worst," opined Ardath.

Bad News

"It's no wonder so many of them can't even get it up without pills," sulked Xoblah. "What are they *doing* to themselves down there?"

Nobody had an answer, nor any idea of what to do about the situation; the solution would require godly wisdom. And as much as Xoblah hated it, she knew Empusa was right; for whatever reason, she had the best chance of presenting the problem to their mistress without provoking one of Her infamous tantrums. And there was no point in putting the ordeal off any longer; it wasn't going to get any easier if she waited.

She soon found the goddess in the garden, having Her hair done by a nymph. As soon as She noticed the succubus, She called out "Why, if it isn't the stormy petrel! And I was so enjoying my afternoon up until now."

Xoblah smiled weakly, and tried to console herself with the thought that perhaps being turned into an incubus and having to deal with mortal *women* for a change wouldn't be so bad. But somehow, she just couldn't bring herself to believe it.

Ladies of the Night

Of all the worlds in all the stories in this book, this may be the most different from our own. At the same time, it was one of the easiest for me to describe because I had already worked it out in detail years ago: it takes place in a universe I designed for a fantasy role-playing game. Interestingly, when it first appeared in my blog a couple of readers seemed to imagine this represented some sort of wish-fulfillment fantasy of mine; apparently they failed to comprehend that not all protagonists need be moral or even sympathetic.

Empathy

Other women cloy the appetites they feed, but she makes hungry where most she satisfies.
- William Shakespeare, *Antony and Cleopatra* (II, ii)

"I'm looking forward to seeing you at seven-ninety then. Thank you, Lord Zolan!" Marilith covered the glass and settled back onto the cushions of the divan; the feelings of a new patron were often overwhelming at first, and she would need much of the next hour to sort through them. "Tea please, Cynthia," she said when her handmaiden appeared in response to the bell.

"Red lotus as usual, mistress?"

"Yes, and the incense too." Then as the servant turned to go, she added, "And you'll need to stay close for this one, I think."

Cynthia's face remained as impassive as ever, but she asked, "Do you think he'll be dangerous?"

"Dangerous? No. Very ardent, though; I can feel his intensity even now, and I'll need your capable hands if I lose myself in so deep a pool." No answer but a deep bow was necessary, so Cynthia gave no other, and a moment later she was gone. Though she had been here for six months now, Marilith was still impressed with her efficiency; she had indeed been a wise investment, just as Dr. Galen had promised.

This house, too, had been a wise investment; its proximity to the palace and the spectacular view of the cloud-piercing Tower of Heaven would have justified its expense even without the space and amenities it offered. As a child, she could only have dreamed of living in Yian, much less owning a lovely mansion and the finest servants human ingenuity could produce…but that was before her talent had manifested itself, and before she had recognized how she could improve her situation by its use.

A wave of lust spread through Marilith's body, momentarily startling her with its intensity; her new client was presently transacting some business in the Tower, and by looking toward it she had inadvertently opened the empathic channel more widely. She inhaled deeply of the calming incense (when had Cynthia brought it in? As silent as she was quick!) and explored Lord Zolan's feelings, gliding through them as though swimming in a strong current, not fighting them yet not allowing them to carry her away, either. He was an important man, high in the Imperial bureaucracy, and such men usually have powerful passions; once she had mapped the rugged and complex landscape of his desires and fully learned how to appeal to them, he would be an excellent and loyal client. Today he would only be here for an hour, but that was almost too much for the first time with such an intense lover.

The tea helped her to master the invading emotions, and when she was done she went to her closet to dress. The contact was more than strong enough for her to divine how best to appeal to him, and by the time his heightened anticipation told her that he was on his way she had dressed, made up and had her hair arranged for maximum effect. All that remained was her customary prayer at the small shrine adjoining her boudoir, and she was ready; when she sensed he had touched down on the landing stage she moved into the parlor and artfully arranged herself on the cushions.

"Lord Zolan of Orissa," Cynthia announced, and he entered the room in a burst of excitement which sharply increased the moment his eyes fell upon Marilith. He crossed

Empathy

the room in a remarkably dignified fashion considering his emotional state, and raised her hand to his lips with something closely akin to awe.

"Your images fall utterly short of the reality," he said in a hoarse whisper. She knew that this was a totally sincere statement; no image, still or moving, could adjust its posture and facial expressions to appeal to the viewer's individual preferences as she had learned to do. She pitied courtesans without her gift; feigned lust and interest, no matter how perfectly imitated, could never match the real ones she borrowed from her clients. She was the perfect dance partner, and followed as effortlessly as a shadow.

Some of her callers relished the anticipation, their passions mounting as she prolonged the preliminaries until the point they could stand it no longer, but Lord Zolan was not one of them; his need was a raging fire, and there would be ample time for conversation once it had been temporarily quenched. For now, only two words were needed: "Take me."

It was as though she had thrown a lever to release some mechanism powered by a tightly-coiled spring. Her own passion rose in tandem with his as he literally tore the gown from her body and covered her bosom in rough kisses, all hope of self-control lost to her now; she wanted him as badly as he wanted her, and there was absolutely nothing artificial about the ecstasy she felt as he entered her, nor about her synchronous climax when he reached his own within a very short time as all her lovers did.

When her senses eventually returned, Marilith glanced at the wall clock and saw it was just after eight; that left ninety minutes of their appointment, so there was no need to awaken her guest right away. While he slept peacefully she could regain her composure and get a better look at him through eyes unblurred by the intense emotions she had felt while he was awake. He was a well-built, good-looking man with strong features, every bit the son of a *sirdar*; according to the peerage records Marilith had consulted last week when he first contacted her, his mother was a great-great granddaughter of the royal house of one of the Outer Worlds. So in addition to the generous fee and the undeniable physical and emotional pleasure she would gain from his visits, he had good family connections on both sides which could prove very valuable to her; his patronage might provide the means by which she eventually secured a title, an advantageous marriage in a class far above that into which she had been born, or both.

But there would be plenty of time for that later; right now she was enjoying her life as the most sought-after companion in the capital…the attention, the intense pleasures, the comforts and most of all the wealth. Political power would come as easily and naturally as the rest had.

She smiled, and began to kiss and caress her noble visitor's head.

Empathy

Ladies of the Night

This is another story whose setting can be pinned down to a fairly specific time, though not an exact day. It's also one of the few in this collection (along with "Ambition", "Dance of the Seasons" and "X Factor") which isn't at all fantastic or science-fictional.

Carnival

Deputy Leclerc pulled his coat closer about him against the icy wind of early Ventôse; how he hated this time of year! It used to be that the beastly weather was made more bearable by the anticipation of Carnival, but the National Assembly had banned it as indecent and the subsequent governments had continued the prohibition, so there was absolutely nothing to ameliorate Leclerc's misery. Ah, well, *c'est la vie*; perhaps someday when the chaos had settled and all corrupt elements had been purged from society, the celebration might be allowed again. He shrugged inwardly; it was best not to think too much about such things, so he turned his attention to avoiding the deeper puddles and quickened his pace a little.

"Why in such a hurry, *Monsieur*?" came a sweet voice from a doorway nearby. "Surely you have a few minutes to tarry with me?" The whore was both young and beautiful, and though her winter clothes disguised her figure somewhat he did not think he would be disappointed when the rest of her charms were revealed. Well, why not? His spirits were in need of lifting, and he could blame any delay on the weather.

Her room was small but comfortable, and though her fee was high for a streetwalker she was clearly no ordinary *fille de joie*; he mused that in less egalitarian times she might've made a courtesan. She certainly had the manners for it, inviting him to remove his boots and warm his feet by the fire while she got him a large mug of bouillon. She then sat with him while he sipped the hot, flavorful broth, making small talk about all manner of subjects while he enjoyed the music of her voice and grunted a response now and again just

109

to keep her going. He soon felt a pleasant drowsiness overcome him, and since he was warm and comfortable and in no hurry to return to the winter outside he did not fight it, but instead drifted into sleep.

He awoke some time later on his back in a dimly-lit room; he felt dizzy, nauseated and weak and it took him several minutes to realize that he had no idea what was going on. He tried to get up and immediately regretted it, then an unfamiliar feminine voice said "I would advise you to lie still for a while, Deputy Leclerc. The embrace of the poppy is not so easily escaped by one unused to her caresses."

A wave of nausea engulfed him as he jerked his head toward the voice, which tutted and then asked "Why do men never listen?" as he proceeded to be violently ill on the dirt floor. When the sickness had subsided he lay back on the straw mat and the strange woman sat down beside him, cleaning his mouth with a wet flannel and feeling his forehead with a soft, warm hand.

"Who are you? Where am I? What is going on here?" he croaked, without waiting for any answers. "Do you know who I am?"

"But of course we know, Deputy Leclerc, which is exactly why you have been brought here. I am your nurse, here to ensure that you are well for your trial in the morning."

"*Trial*? He asked incredulously; "By what authority do you presume to put a deputy of the National Convention on trial?"

"Why, by the same authority that we all presumed to storm the Bastille and set up our own government, namely the natural right of all men and women to liberty and equality."

Carnival

"The National Convention is the duly elected government of the Republic, and only the Committee of Public Safety has the right to administer justice!"

"In the opinions of many, the Convention lost its mandate to govern women when it sent our champion, Madame De Gouges, to the guillotine."

"Many? What many?" he scoffed.

"You will see in the morning," she said, and would not elaborate further.

Leclerc did not sleep well, though neither his nurse nor his accommodations could be faulted for that. No, it was the reference to Olympe de Gouges which worried him. Could he be in the hands of the remnants of the Girondist party? If so, his time on Earth was nearly over; he did not think they would be as averse to bloodshed now as they had been in the past. He tried to engage his nurse in conversation, to no avail; she had apparently said all she wished to say and showed admirable restraint thereafter.

But the morning eventually came, and his nurse was replaced by a woman who presented a basin and ewer and bade him make himself presentable, followed by another who brought him a generous breakfast. Soon after he was finished the door was opened and Leclerc wondered if he might not be suffering some aftereffect of the opium with which the whore had drugged him, because into the room came two tall women dressed as Amazon warriors! He started to laugh but it soon died in his throat because their spears were quite real and the scowls on their faces quite serious. They ushered him out of the room and though he considered making a break for it he realized that he had no idea where he was and no way of knowing the way to the exit.

Ladies of the Night

In a few moments he realized he must be in some portion of the *Carrières de Paris* which had been renovated to include rooms and at least one large chamber into which he was now led; the rough walls of the former mine were covered with decorative hangings and the space was ringed with wooden benches crowded with spectators. A jury box lay on his right, and directly ahead of him a judge's bench and witness stand. All of the seats were already occupied; he was the last participant to arrive. He was astonished to note that he was the only normally-dressed person there; everyone else, from judge to prosecutor to jurors to spectators, were all arrayed in colorful costumes far more suited to a Carnival celebration than to a courtroom. And as he surveyed the scene, he noticed something far more disquieting; every single masked face he could see was that of a woman.

The trial was like a nightmare; he heard his own voice pleading not guilty to the charges, saw himself standing and sitting and answering as he was bidden, listened to the women in their outlandish attire give evidence against him, and heard the damning recitation of his misdeeds against humanity in general and women in particular not merely for the past few years, but stretching back through his whole debauched life. And as the testimony unfolded a common thread became apparent to him, revealed by the nature of the charges and the details of the witnesses' accounts: Every one of them was a whore. He fancied that he recognized the judge and prosecutor beneath their masks as well-known courtesans, and it was not too difficult to guess that jurors and spectators were all *demimondaines* as well. He realized now that he had misinterpreted the nurse's calling Olympe de Gouges "our champion"; before she had become an advocate for the rights of women, a Girondist sympathizer and an outspoken critic of the increasingly-common executions, the

Carnival

noted writer had been a courtesan. The *demimonde* apparently considered her one of its own, and the judge honored the great lady's aversion to violence by sentencing Leclerc to a peaceful death by overdose of opium.

Ladies of the Night

I feel it only fair to warn you: this story is very strange. It's similar to "Mercy" in that it's a quasi-sequel, a story which could have taken place in the world of one of my favorite tales (in this case, a movie) had things gone just a little differently. I think most of you will probably pick up on it pretty quickly, and if you don't you might be inclined to read the comments on my blog for August 23rd, 2012.

Friend

Greta ground the butt of the cigarette into the ashtray, then opened her case for another. Upon realizing that she only had four left and wasn't sure when she would be able to get more, she decided to conserve them. She didn't normally smoke as much as she had tonight, but she was unusually nervous; her instincts told her something was very wrong, and they never lied. Perhaps it was the way Klaus had behaved when he let her know this group was on the way last night; perhaps it was the unusually large size, more than twice as many as usual. Maybe it was the one little girl who simply would *not* stop crying, or the heavy rain.

But most likely, it was the fact that Albert was an unprecedented three hours late.

Ignoring the silent question in the refugees' eyes, she went back upstairs, put on her coat and hat and went onto the balcony with her binoculars. It was a futile gesture, really; in this weather she wouldn't be able to see anything outside her own grounds. But it kept her occupied for at least a few minutes, and allowed her to avoid the frightened people downstairs who might be able to read the apprehension on her features.

After returning the wet things to the rack she went to Goliath's room at the end of the hall, knocked and let herself in; she found him where she knew she would, seated in his massive wooden chair staring out at the storm with a strange look of fascination. When she touched his hand he turned to her and smiled that silly grin of his, and perceiving his empty tray she asked, "Was your supper good?"

"Yes. Very good," he said.

Ladies of the Night

"I'm glad. It shouldn't be much longer now, then we'll have the house to ourselves again."

"Good," he frowned. "I hate crowds."

"I know you do," said Greta, "but what we're doing is very important. These people are trying to escape bad men who want to capture them, to lock them in chains and maybe even kill them. The bad men hate them because they're different, and you know what that's like, don't you?"

"Yes," he said quietly, with incredible sadness. "I know."

Greta was fairly sure he did. Her father had taken him in over 20 years ago after his previous caretaker had died of influenza, and though he was simple and childlike, his great size and terribly ugly features frightened people so much the family kept him hidden as much as possible. "I'm going to leave your door ajar, so you can hear if there's trouble, all right?" He didn't answer, but she knew he understood.

She found the leader of the little group waiting for her at the bottom of the stairs. "What can I do for you, Rabbi?"

"I wanted to thank you on behalf of my people, for endangering yourself to help us."

"Greta is just a stage name, Rabbi; my mother called me Judith."

"Ah. Then you are in as much danger as we are should you be found out; why do you not escape to Switzerland yourself?"

"Guilt. At first I was as happy to take their money as I was to take that of any other man, and even more so after the Nuremberg Laws made them all criminals for hiring me. But after the war started and the usual hate turned into something monstrous, I knew what manner of men I had

Friend

entertained and I feel I will never be clean of their foul touch."

"Yet their money paid for our refuge, and your profession gave you the contacts you have used to help so many of your people, just as Rahab sheltered Joshua's men in Jericho," he said. "Think about that."

Before Greta could answer there was a squeal of brakes followed by the sounds of running feet and a pounding on her door; she saw shadows flitting past the windows and knew that disaster had come upon them. The door flew open, and in strode a Gestapo officer, announcing that everyone was under arrest; in moments several of his men had entered the room. There were not many but they were armed and organized, and thus more than a match for a group of panicked refugees, most of them women and children.

They were no match, however, for the nightmare that came lumbering down the stairs a moment later, ignoring their bullets as completely as he ignored the officer's frantic orders to halt. Goliath flung aside the first men he encountered as easily as an angry child might fling a doll, and both refugees and Gestapo alike screamed in terror when he put his right hand on the officer's shoulder and in one quick motion *tore his head off* with the left.

Greta knew it was imperative she get the refugees away from the melee; in his berserk state Goliath might not be able to tell friend from foe, and might perceive screaming and panic as a threat. "The back door!" she shouted. "Out the back door!" The Nazis who had originally gone around to block that way had immediately returned to the front when the screaming started, though they would soon wish they hadn't. Once outside, she directed the fleeing group toward the barn and then made a wide circle around to the front herself, hoping to calm Goliath down once the battle came to its inevitable conclusion.

Only once before had Greta been directly exposed to her protector's incredible capacity for violence; years ago a client had turned brutal and, summoned by her screams, Goliath had burst through the door and literally dismembered her assailant. But that incident had been over before it started; this was carnage on a scale she had never even imagined. Body parts lay strewn madly about, the windowpanes were opaque with blood and Goliath was stumbling around the front lawn in the pouring rain, growling and crying out incoherently and swinging a grisly club (which Greta took to be a human shin) at invisible, airborne opponents.

"I'm safe!" she shouted at him, "Look, it's me, Judith! Your friend! The bad men didn't hurt me!" He heard, and turned toward her with a look of such implacable fury that for a moment she was terrified he could not recognize her.

But then his features softened abruptly; he dropped his grotesque weapon, reached out toward her with open hands and plaintively called out, "Friend?"

"Yes, it's me, I'm all right! You did good, you protected the people! But the battle is over now, and you have to be calm again." But as she spoke, she realized he was looking past her and scowling, and she turned to discover that several of the men had come up behind her after arming themselves with the dead Nazis' guns. "He won't hurt you!" she cried. "He only attacks people who threaten him or me."

Friend

"Do you know what that is?" one of the older men shouted. "It's…"

"It is a golem!" interrupted the Rabbi, in a voice that commanded attention. "Do you not know the story of Rabbi Judah Loew of Prague, who created a man-like creature from inanimate matter in order to defend the Jews? This is another like it."

His authoritative declaration had the desired effect; the guns went down, albeit slowly, and Greta suggested it would be better for them to wait in the barn with their families while she tried to discover whether Albert had been captured or merely delayed. In either case, they would have to leave soon, and this time she and Goliath would go with them; this place wasn't safe for anyone now.

"Come on," she said, as calmly as she could manage. "We both need to get out of these wet things." And with that she took his huge hand in hers, and led him back into their home for the last time.

Ladies of the Night

Though this story is a light fantasy and its setting intentionally non-specific, the police commissioner's remarks about the pressures put upon Southeast Asian countries by the American government describe a very real situation. Sex workers in those countries are routinely subjected to terrible mistreatment by the police in order to cater to American notions of morality, and though the sex workers in this story get help in resisting the abuse, those in real life will continue to be harmed for as long as the current moral panic over "sex trafficking" continues. Both Human Rights Watch and sex worker rights groups (especially in Thailand and Cambodia) have extensively documented the pogroms, and several UN agencies have called for the decriminalization of prostitution in order to remove the excuse police use to beat, rob, rape and torture women who are trying to make a living in the best way available to them.

Genius Loci

The southwest furthers.
The northeast does not further.
It furthers one to see the great man.
Perseverance brings good fortune. - *I Ching*, hexagram 39

Every policeman in Central Headquarters had avoided the Chief Inspector yesterday; he had arrived at work in a nastier mood than usual, collected a number of files and then left on a trip to the capital to meet with the Commissioner of Police. And though he had abominably maltreated everyone who had the misfortune to cross his path, nobody really blamed him because they knew the reason for that meeting. And now, as the Chief Inspector waited to be called in to his superior's office, he was fervently wishing that he could be almost anyplace but here.

Fortunately, he did not have long to wait; he was admitted to the beautifully-appointed office he had last seen just after his promotion five years ago and bowed deeply. The Commissioner acknowledged him with a perfunctory nod, gestured toward a chair in front of his desk, and began speaking as soon as he was seated.

"As I told you in our communication yesterday, I have observed a most strange anomaly in the figures for prostitution arrests in your city," he began, pointing at a computer screen to his left. "You assured me that you could explain, but that it would be better for you to do so in person. Accordingly, I have made time for you in my busy schedule. Please proceed."

The Commissioner always spoke that way. He was a former Professor of Criminology, renowned for his erudition and problem-solving ability, and had been rewarded for years of distinguished service with this choice political appointment. So although he was not a large man, he could be extremely intimidating, especially to a lower official with an apparently-insurmountable problem. "Yes, sir. Well, sir, I'm afraid I must begin by telling you that the situation is actually worse than the official figures make it appear."

"Oh?" he asked, with the barest trace of annoyance. "Considering that your city has the largest red-light district in the entire country, yet for the past several years has had the lowest number of prostitution arrests by a considerable margin, I am at a loss to understand how it *could* be worse."

He swallowed hard. "Well, sir, those arrest figures have actually been, ah, inflated somewhat. They're not even as high as reported."

"And how many have there been, *actually*?" That last word was as menacing as a gun-barrel.

"Um, well, it's been dropping for a long time, and in the past six months there have been very few, but then this month we reached an all-time low of, ah, none."

"*None whatsoever?*"

"No, sir."

"Considering that your performance of your duties has been exemplary in every other way, I am absolutely certain you have some credible explanation for your pronounced deficiency in this particular area. As you well know, our foreign aid from the Americans requires the production of sufficient human trafficking arrests to satisfy their moral crusade."

"Yes, sir, I'm aware of that, and when I first took over the post from my predecessor I noticed the numbers were quite low and resolved to correct the situation. So I increased the number of raids, and instituted harsh discipline against any man caught taking bribes from the madams. Yet still, the numbers kept shrinking, for no discernible reason."

"What do you mean, 'no discernible reason'? Surely all the prostitutes didn't mysteriously vanish?"

"But that's just it, sir; it was as though they *had*. Whenever I sent a squad out to raid a brothel, they found it locked and shuttered. When officers were dispatched to a bar, they found only men drinking. When they went to bring in street women, they found all the usual areas deserted. Even when informants told us of activity taking place, it was not so by the time we arrived. It was as though someone was warning them that we were on the way."

"Obviously, the pimps and madams have a confederate inside your office."

"That was what I thought at first, sir, so I tried not announcing the raids; I would just suddenly come in, order a group of men to follow me, and take them to the red light district myself. I found the same thing that had been reported to me: locked doors and deserted streets. I assumed that it was a trick, and that there was some secret way of gaining admittance; so we started breaking down doors, only to find the buildings empty. Yet my informants told me they were doing a thriving trade again the next day, all doors and windows open."

The Commissioner no longer appeared angry; now he was the professor again, considering the complexities of an abstruse problem. "What did you do next?"

"I reshuffled the entire department, bringing new staff into my office and reassigning the entire vice squad. Then I took officers from other divisions on the raids, to no avail; the numbers continued to drop. Every arrest we have had in the past year was obtained by officers bringing in known prostitutes who were buying groceries, eating in restaurants or riding in public conveyances, or else beggars we charged with prostitution to hide our disgrace."

"Do you have any theory at all to explain this strange phenomenon?"

"Yes, sir, but I was afraid to tell you lest you think me mad."

Now the Commissioner was intrigued. "Do go on."

"Well, sir, I asked the same question of all my senior officers; I even promised a promotion to the one who could explain it. Finally a group of them came to me one afternoon, and told me that they knew *exactly* what was responsible."

He hesitated for so long the Commissioner finally spurred him on with, "Yes…?"

"It's because of, um, a spirit."

"*A spirit*?!?"

"Yes, sir."

"Do you *actually* expect me to believe that the ghost of some dead prostitute is going around warning her colleagues about our raids in time for them to flee?"

"Well, not exactly, sir. I mean, yes and no. We don't think she's that kind of spirit." This time the Commissioner did not prod him, so he swallowed and went on. "You see, sir, I was so desperate by this point that I was willing to try anything, so I brought in a priest to perform an exorcism."

"A novel solution to a novel problem, but clearly it failed."

"I'm afraid so, sir. The priest went to the red-light district, and talked to the prostitutes, and performed some sort of spiritual investigation, including research in many books. And then he came to me and said, 'I cannot help you;

124

this is not a restless spirit reluctant to be reborn, but rather the guardian spirit of the area. As such, it would be wrong for me to attempt to drive it out even if I could.' I know this priest, sir; he is a wise and holy man, and I trust his judgment on this matter."

The Commissioner thought for a moment. "This district has been associated with the flesh trade for centuries, yet nobody has ever seen this spirit before."

"Well, sir, that's not exactly true. Part of the priest's research was historical, and he showed me records telling that though the spirit has never appeared during a time when prostitution was tolerated, it has often been seen during periods of intolerance. In fact, the priest warned me that the manifestations would become more powerful, and more dangerous to my men, should we persist in harassing the women and their business."

The Commissioner grew quiet. He turned in his chair to look out at the rain; then he rose and paced back and forth for a few minutes. Several times he looked as though he were about to ask a question, then thought better of it. After a while he sat down and worked on his computer, intently examining the data displayed on the screen. Then he turned sideways in the chair again, fixing his eyes on one of the awards on his wall, and sat quietly for a time. The Chief Inspector did nothing to disturb him; he merely prayed silently, grateful he had not been fired on the spot.

Finally, the Commissioner spoke. "We will turn this to our advantage. First, you will announce that the human traffickers have grown so dangerous, you can no longer allow representatives of NGOs to go into the red-light district unless accompanied by a police officer; if this spirit warns the prostitutes of our approach, that will allow us to later demonstrate to the Americans that we have 'cleaned up' the district, since there will never be any prostitutes about when they go to look."

"A brilliant idea, sir! But, won't they want to see the women we've 'rescued'?"

"I was coming to that. I will announce – completely unrelated to your announcement, of course – that we are expanding opportunities for women in the police force, and will begin actively recruiting them immediately. This will also please the Americans, who will no doubt provide some grant to help us train them. We will then disguise the new policewomen as prostitutes, send them out to the district, pretend to arrest them, and send them to a new 'rehabilitation center'; we will keep NGO members away from the center due to 'concern for the women's privacy' so they can't discover that it is a false front. Then we send the same women out again to be 'arrested' again, until we can credibly claim to have 'rescued' a large fraction of them. The Americans will be happy; our government will collect more money; you will be lauded as a champion against trafficking; the prostitutes will be free to work in peace; the men will be able to hire them without fear of exposure; and the spirit will be placated."

"Magnificent! What a plan!" the Inspector cried, rising spontaneously to his feet. "I am a fool for not having brought this problem to you sooner."

"Nonsense. You are a practical man, trained to deal with mortal criminals; it would be unreasonable of me to blame you for fearing my reaction."

The Chief Inspector, now smiling like a child with a new toy, bowed excitedly, thanked the Commissioner again, gathered up his documents and set forth to implement the new plan, relieved of the burden under which he had struggled for so long. And once he had gone, the Commissioner silently thanked the Buddha for a most interesting mental exercise and asked his secretary to bring him a pot of tea.

Ladies of the Night

Don't waste your time trying to figure out where or when this story takes place; some things look the same no matter which direction one views them from.

Palindrome

A character is like an acrostic or Alexandrian stanza; read it forward, backward, or across, it still spells the same thing. - Ralph Waldo Emerson

The dream had been so lovely; Anna was walking barefoot across a field of wildflowers along the verge of a wood, not in a park but in some unspoiled place without fences, signs or crowds. The sun was shining on her face and birds were singing, and she came across a stag caught by his antlers in a thicket. He was absolutely magnificent, but all his great strength was useless against the bramble in which he had become entwined. She knew that if she left him there he would soon become easy prey for some predator, so she moved slowly, gingerly toward him, intending to pull the thorns away with her bare hands if necessary so he might go free. But just as she reached out for the nearest of the vines, she was shocked awake by the slamming of the outer door and the braying voice of the guard announcing breakfast.

It was the same thing every day. There was no earthly reason why any of them needed to wake up at a particular time; it wasn't like the food was hot or worth getting up for, and even if one of them was going to be released or transferred that rarely happened before noon. It was just part of the petty sadism which characterized nearly every prison procedure, like the lights being kept on all night and the prisoners being reshuffled every few days to keep friendships from forming. Anna tried not to let it break her down; for example, once the guard had left she would simply cover her head again and go back to sleep, letting the others take what they wanted from her breakfast tray. But today

129

was different; the guard actually came into the cell and shook her roughly.

"Get up, Cleopatra; you're rolling out this morning." The guards had lots of stupid, mocking nicknames for her; she tried to ignore that as well. But the rest of that statement was definitely unexpected.

"What do you mean, rolling out?"

"Just what I said, Princess; your presence has been requested elsewhere."

Anna knew better than to inquire further; if she expressed any interest at all the guard would refuse to answer on principle. She'd find out soon enough. For a moment she wondered if this might not be some sort of mental torture, but quickly realized the guards didn't have that kind of imagination. Then she dared to think for a moment that she might have been paroled, but immediately strangled the idea before it could grow into a hope. It was better just to wait and expect the worst.

Four and a half hours later, the wait finally ended; the guard came back and told her to stand, roughly jerking her by the arm without waiting for her to get up on her own. She was then hustled to an anteroom and given back her own clothes, the ones she was wearing when she was arrested; they were wrinkled and had a musty odor, but she still preferred them to the horrible, shapeless prison uniform and so she eagerly exchanged the latter for the former, heedless of the guards she knew were leering at her through the two-way mirror.

She then exited through the far end of the room as instructed, where she was met by one of the dress-uniform guards who interacted with government officials and the like; next to her was a woman in a lab coat, accompanied by what Anna assumed was an orderly. So that's what this was about;

Palindrome

she had been committed to a psychiatric facility. She wasn't surprised, and was in fact relieved; the treatment there couldn't be any worse than it was here.

And indeed, it wasn't. The nurse was friendly and the orderly didn't bully her; the ride was long and peaceful and Anna slept for most of it, and when the nurse woke her it was with a gentle shake rather than the slam of a door. The state hospital at the end of the journey was still a prison, of course; the doors were just as locked and the guards just as vigilant, but she had a private room with a soft bed and the lights were actually turned off at night. The food was good and she was able to eat sitting at a real table in the cafeteria rather than from a tray in her lap; there was even a little park, thought it was surrounded on all sides by the walls of the huge facility.

For a whole week, she was largely left to her own devices; she listened to music and read books from the ward's library, and every night they screened a movie. Other than the locked doors and the rigid schedule, the only real reminders that she was in a hospital were the various medical tests and questionnaires to which she was subjected, and the technicians were always polite and friendly. It was so nice, in fact, that Anna began to think that if it weren't for the lack of privacy this might not be a bad place for a holiday.

Then on the morning of the ninth day, the chief ward nurse told her that she had been assigned a doctor and would start her therapy that afternoon. Anna actually found herself looking forward to that; everyone else here was so pleasant, she couldn't imagine the doctor being less so. For the first time, she allowed herself to accept the idea that maybe it might be nice to be cured of her problem, to be able to live like everybody else and form normal relationships as her

Ladies of the Night

friends did. Perhaps it might even be possible for her to eventually forgive Eve for turning her in; after all, she had done it because she was worried about Anna, and was clearly remorseful when she found out about the brutal way her friend had been treated by the police.

Dr. Lil was a somewhat plump, maternal woman in late middle age, and Anna instantly liked her; she therefore resolved that she would cooperate in every way possible so as to hasten the day when she could rejoin society as a healthy, functioning member, and told the doctor so.

"How wonderful!" she said with genuine emotion. "I'm so very glad to hear you say that, Anna; you see, it was I who initiated the process to have you transferred here. I reviewed your case history and interviewed your friends, and I could clearly see you weren't an incorrigible deviant." She opened the folder to refresh her memory. "Now, in school you never showed any signs of perversion; when did you first start feeling sexual attraction to men?"

(With grateful acknowledgement to Charles Beaumont).

Palindrome

Ladies of the Night

You may have noticed in the last story that Anna isn't overtly a prostitute; that's because I was intentionally vague about many of the details of her world. I suggest you go back and reread the first paragraph, then ask yourself A) how men are treated in this world, and B) how Anna came to be arrested. This next story isn't about a pro at all, but it revolves around a possible drawback to one "solution" prohibitionists have proposed (see my blog of May 6th, 2012) for the so-called "problem" of prostitution.

Rose

O Rose thou art sick.
The invisible worm
That flies in the night
In the howling storm
Has found out thy bed
Of crimson joy
And his dark secret love
Does thy life destroy. - William Blake

No matter how long I'm with Jerry, I never fail to get excited when he comes home from a business trip! I always put extra effort into making sure the house is clean from top to bottom and end to end, and I always fix him something really special for dinner, one of those dishes that takes a lot of extra work. This time I decided to do a Greek *moussaka*; I found some really lovely eggplants at the grocery, and I have everything timed perfectly so he won't have to wait long after he gets home. Jerry always hates for dinner to be late, but he *especially* hates it when he arrives from travel because he won't eat airline food, so he'll be ravenous. Poor dear! I'm so very fortunate not to have to travel farther than the shops; being banged around on public conveyances always upsets me so.

Over the past few days I've really had time to think, and I believe I've come up with the perfect plan for rekindling his interest. I suppose it was inevitable that his eyes and mind would begin to stray after a while; it's the way men are constructed, after all, and one can't blame any creature for following its programming! At the same time it hurts every time I catch him looking at some gorgeous

135

Ladies of the Night

model, and perhaps fantasizing that he might replace me with her.

Well, that's all going to stop! Since we've already explored every fantasy he had and a few he discovered on the video, something new was called for. So I went online to talk to some of my friends, and to ask their advice; Daisy gave me the address of this site with all manner of sex tips and tricks, and even a function which uses the activities and fantasies a person enjoys to predict other ones he might like. And I think I've got one that will really impress him! After dinner and coffee I'll massage his feet while he watches a few shows, and when it's time I'll spring it on him.

Jerry doesn't like my going online any more than I absolutely have to; he says it isn't safe, that there is some really horrible malware out there right now, and that if I do go online I should stick only to established, well-known sites. So I'm sure he'd be angry with me if I told him where I picked up my new bedroom activities, but I think he'll be so happy he won't think to ask…and if he does ask later, I'll just have to take the consequences. I don't mind losing a few privileges for a while if it revives our relationship.

Still, it's pretty frustrating to have to do all this. It's not like I haven't worked hard to please him for the past ten years; I still look exactly as I always have, and I can see the men staring at me whenever I go into town. Everything in the house is always immaculate, and I'm very careful to keep up the maintenance schedule so nothing breaks down when he needs it. I even took the time to learn about his ex-wife's bad habits so as to be *absolutely sure* I didn't accidentally copy them. I give him everything he wants in bed, and everything he wants at table, and I've never embarrassed him in front of his friends, not even that awful Warren who can't keep his hands to himself. And after all that, for him to still

Rose

get tired of me…well, it hurts, a lot. And then this morning on the phone, I found out that he's been travelling with a woman, his new secretary, and I could just tell she was one of those little sluts who will use her sex appeal to wrap the boss around her little finger. It made me so upset I actually broke a plate…not on purpose, of course, but it's still the first one I've *ever* broken, and that snapped me back to myself right away.

I honestly don't know what's wrong with me; why do I feel this way? I've never been one to behave erratically or to cause trouble, not even on the rare occasions when I've come down with a virus or something. Ever since yesterday I've been so agitated that it actually frightens me; I don't even have a *word* for this feeling! Well, after tonight I won't have to worry about it; I'll surprise Jerry with my new technique, and he'll fall in love with me all over again, and we'll live happily ever after.

"Are you sure she's safe, Doc?"

"Perfectly. I deleted the past three days of her memory and set her inhibitor software to maximum; she doesn't really comprehend what's going on and literally couldn't hurt a fly now."

"But why don't you just shut her down completely?"

"Because the Bellaflora series has a volatile operating system; it's part of what lets them mimic human behavior so perfectly. If I shut her down, we won't be able to analyze her to find out what happened…and given that there are about 1500 of her model in this city alone, I'd say it's pretty important that we do, don't you?"

Ladies of the Night

The detective looked around at the blood-spattered furniture, the medics carrying out their grisly burden in a plastic bag, the forensic team pointlessly gathering evidence that would never be used because the murderer was not in question; the meat cleaver was still in her hand when they arrived. "Yeah, I'd say. But Doc, what the hell *did* happen?"

He sighed, rubbed the bridge of his nose and pulled out a pill case, offering the detective one as well. "Ever seen any really old science fiction?" he asked.

"What, like 20th-century stuff? Not really. My wife is the classic film buff; I like comedies."

"Way back when robots were just a science fiction concept, still many decades in the future, one common trope was that they would have no emotions; in fact, plots often hinged on the idea that emotions are what defines a human. Of course, that's bunk; emotions are really primitive things, not a specifically human characteristic at all. Any fish can feel fear, any snake anger. And if there's a love more pure and perfect than that of a dog, we've never discovered it. No, emotions are easy to program; they're reflexive and automatic, and can be installed as firmware. Abstract reasoning, moral judgment...*those* are the cognitive functions that define a human, and we haven't come up with a really good artificial simulation of them yet."

"But Doc, if that's true, why aren't robots committing murders all the time?"

"Because *we* choose which emotions to give them, and of course it's always things like love, loyalty, happiness, pride of accomplishment, that sort of thing. Even guard robots are motivated by loyalty to their charges, not aggression."

"Then how..." the detective trailed off.

138

Rose

"It looks like somebody figured out how to simulate jealousy, and to install it via a worm; she probably picked it up from some dodgy website." Then, turning to the gynoid sitting quietly in her chair, he said, "Come along, Rose."

"But Dr. Morton, I have to wait for Jerry; he'll be home in a few hours, and your boys have made an awful mess of the place."

"Jerry's been delayed, dear; he asked me to tell you he won't be home until Friday, and said I could borrow you to help with some research I'm doing."

Her face broke into a bright, happy smile. "Oh, I'm very good at assisting and organizing! I always do exactly as I'm programmed, with a very high degree of thoroughness and efficiency!"

"I know that, Rose," he said sadly. "I've seen your work."

Ladies of the Night

I wrote the first version of this story in 1987 or '88, but I was not at all happy with it; it was too slow (which is saying something in a short-short) and too blah. I tried rewriting it several times in the '90s, to no avail; it would simply never gel so I put it down as a failure. Then just a few weeks after I wrote "The Trick", this one popped back into my head and I realized that what it needed was for the heroine to be a courtesan and the action to be placed 100 years or so earlier. The result is one of my favorites.

Painted Devil

'Tis the eye of childhood that fears a painted devil. - William Shakespeare, *Macbeth* (II, ii)

Monique took the hand of the coachman and lightly stepped down with a "Thank you, Pierre."

"Will you be requiring the coach again today, Madame?"

"No, Pierre, I cancelled my appointments for today because of the funeral; I'm sure my gentlemen will understand."

"Very good, Madame. Please accept my condolences on the death of Monsieur Dupuy; I know he was a good and generous friend to you."

"Thank you, Pierre; Monsieur Dupuy was as generous in death as in life, for he has left me his entire estate."

"Small condolence for the loss of such a fine gentleman, Madame."

His words were true and honest, and she smiled at him before turning to enter her house. Pierre was exactly right; though she appreciated Francois Dupuy's generosity, it was scarce comfort for the loss of a man who had been both a steadfast friend and a reliable client for over twenty-five years. Monique had known him since adopting her trade in her late teens, and he had assisted her with his money, cleverness and connections many times in the ensuing years; she was certain she would never have made it through the War, the Occupation and the Reconstruction without his help.

But now he was gone, and though the lawyer had made it clear that her late patron's estate was more than large enough to support her in the manner to which she had

141

become accustomed for the rest of her natural life, Monique
could not help but wish that she could turn back the clock
and somehow prevent the acute apoplectic seizure which had
claimed Francois a few days ago. And though she had long
known he had no living family, it had never occurred to
Monique that she might inherit his considerable wealth,
probably because she relied on his always being there despite
his advanced age.

"How old was Monsieur Dupuy, Madame?" asked
Camille as though she could read her mistress' mind.

"I'm not sure," Monique said as she handed the maid
her hat and gloves; "older than he seemed, of that I am
certain. He seemed to me not more than perhaps sixty, but
though he was a native of the city he once mentioned having
been born a Spanish citizen, so he must have been over
eighty."

"A good and full life, God rest him. I know I can
speak for the others in saying we will all miss him, Madame,
both for his kindness to us and his loyalty to you."

"Thank you, Camille. Please let Giselle know that I
don't want a hot dinner this evening, just a little bread and
cheese."

Monique spent the remaining daylight in her garden;
she tried to read but soon found it impossible, so she
contented herself with listening to the birds and the street
noises beyond the wall, and watching the squirrels collecting
acorns for the approaching winter. As she sat her mind kept
returning to the mystery of her friend's life; she knew he had
been a businessman who was invested in so many different
industries that the bad times of the sixties and seventies
which had ruined so many others had proved little more than
an annoyance to him. He had seen her once a week without
fail for over a quarter of a century, and had helped her to

arrange her affairs so carefully that even during those black days when she lost most of her business she still had enough to pay her bills and retain her staff. Political difficulties defeated him no more than economic ones; he was never troubled even by the Beast Butler, and his cloak of immunity was extended to Monique while the other courtesans were having a very bad time.

He was also an accomplished painter, scholar and natural philosopher, and had fascinated her by explaining such diverse subjects as theosophical ideas, Darwin's theory and the principle behind the telephone in terms she could understand. He had also frequently engaged her in discussions of various moral and philosophical topics which had broadened her outlook considerably beyond that of many of her contemporaries. In more fanciful moments she had imagined him as a wizard out of legend, and indeed he had often performed feats of scientific legerdemain to entertain guests at her parties. As she thought of those happy times now, she found herself weeping for the first time today; here in her garden she could at last openly express her grief for the loss of the man who had been her patron, teacher and protector.

Between her professional engagements and the disposition of Francois' effects, the next few weeks were busy ones for her; besides all of the mundane possessions to be sold, the art objects to be displayed and the specimens to be donated to museums, there were a multitude of items which defied categorization, many of which she felt it better to leave to experts. But eventually there were only a few items of furniture left, including a large, shallow cedar wardrobe whose key had apparently been mislaid. Since it was too beautiful to risk breaking she had summoned a locksmith, and after he opened it she asked her butler Gaston to pay him while she examined the mysterious contents of the musty cabinet; they consisted entirely of what appeared to be a framed painting wrapped in badly-aged velvet.

It turned out to be a portrait of a young and handsome gentleman, dressed in the Parisian style of just over a century earlier. She was quite familiar with Francois' technique and this was most assuredly not of his workmanship; in fact, she had never seen a portrait executed with such eerily perfect detail. It was almost more like a photograph than a painting, only in color and endowed with the depth and character so conspicuously lacking in photographs. But as she stood admiring the work of the unknown master who had created it, she was horrified to see the face of the painted Frenchman turn slightly in her direction and even more horrified to *hear him speak!*

"Madame, I thank you for freeing me from the confines of that dark cupboard! Allow me to introduce myself; my name is Guillame de Montaigne, and I was imprisoned in this painting by sorcerous means in order to effect the theft of my property. I have not seen the light of day since those foul cloths were first draped over me, and pardon my boldness but I am compelled to say I could not have wished for a lovelier vision after all that time."

His French was impeccable, and she could well believe that the speaker was a nobleman of pre-revolutionary days. But his fine and flowery words could not distract Monique from the absolute *wrongness* of the experience; for a mere image to speak thus defied every natural law, and she could not help but believe that if Francois had wanted this being released from his canvas prison he would have somehow found the means to do so long before. "If this is true, why were you never freed by the previous owner of the portrait, a good and noble man far wiser in the ways of the world than I?" Her French grammar was as good as his, though colored by a colonial accent.

"Perhaps he knew not the contents of the wardrobe?" the figure suggested helpfully. "In any case, it would take no great wisdom to release me; only speak aloud the inscription on the frame below me."

Monique's eyes automatically dropped to the Latin inscription of which he spoke, but some inner voice warned her to avert her gaze before she reached the end; after all, she only had this creature's word the inscription need be read aloud, and with the cynicism of her profession she was not inclined to trust him. "If Monsieur will forgive my being equally bold as himself, why should I do this? What would it profit me?"

His eyes narrowed, and Monique fancied she now noted a hint of cruelty in them; then he chuckled and said, "Ah, so I am dealing with a woman of custom! Name your price, and I swear I will pay it immediately upon my release."

"I have never before performed this sort of service, and know not the customary price."

He chuckled again, "And a shrewd one as well! As you have discerned I am not without magical powers, and indeed was only defeated by trickery. Very well then, you shall have riches beyond those of anyone else in your nation."

Monique shrugged. "I was already wealthy before my good patron passed beyond this world, and he has endowed me with more than I could spend in ten lifetimes."

Ladies of the Night

"Very well, then, power; I shall make you a noblewoman, even a queen."

"You have indeed slept long, *Monsieur la peinture*; we do not have nobles in this country, nor in yours any longer either. And none of their power kept their heads and necks together once the mob declared it should be otherwise. Besides, no right-thinking man wants power over his fellows, and despite what some of your sex claim we women are no less capable of moral judgment."

The eyes narrowed again, and Monique detected the faintest hint of desperation in the voice. "Youth, then! You are still quite beautiful, Madame, but unless I have lost my eye for woman you are above forty, and despite your best efforts the ravages of age will not be kept at bay for many years longer."

His words penetrated her like a dagger; she knew full well that he spoke truly, and that ere long not even the most expensive cosmetics nor the most advanced treatments of modern medicine would serve to arrest the aging process. But she now knew with certainty that this creature was a thing unholy, and that no good could possibly come of a bargain with him no matter how tempting the reward. So she said simply, "Age and death come to all, and I have enjoyed the benefits of comeliness longer and more thoroughly than most of my sisters."

Truly desperate now, the figure barked "Love then! Your sisters have husbands to comfort them in their old age, *Madame la courtisane*, but not you, I think. I shall secure the permanent affections of the man of your choice for you!"

Monique then laughed, a true and honest laugh of relief. She curtsied to the portrait and said, "I thank you, Monsieur, for teaching me that devils are no wiser than mortal men. For you must be a very great fool indeed if you hope to gain advantage over one of my profession with the promise of love." She then returned the velvet to its place around the painting; the image's scream was suddenly cut off the moment the drape fell into place as though the spell had been broken. She then bound it with cords and shouted, "Gaston!"

He appeared in moments with a worried look. "Yes, Madame?"

"Burn this foul thing in the garbage pit at once; it offends my eyes!"

"At once, Madame!" Gaston did not question; she followed him down to the yard, watched as he doused it liberally with oil and set it alight, then kept vigil late into the night until the last ember had faded. Monique did not know why Francois had never destroyed the painting himself; she could not believe he was unaware of its presence in the wardrobe, so perhaps he was somehow *unable* to destroy it. But whatever the reason, Monique at last felt as though she had repaid her dear friend a little of his unending kindness, and in some small way earned her legacy.

Ladies of the Night

We think of the characters of mythology as being locked in the milieu *of whatever culture produced those myths, but if they were truly immortal surely they should have survived into the present? And though the gods may have moved on to other worlds when this one decided it no longer needed them, those beings of only semi-divine status might have had to make more pragmatic arrangements.*

Pearls Before Swine

...as soon as she heard me she came down, opened the door, and asked me to come in...she set me on a richly decorated seat inlaid with silver, there was a footstool also under my feet, and she mixed...a golden goblet for me to drink... – Homer, *Odyssey* (X)

By the time the black-and-white car had come to a stop in front of the grand old house, the girl on the porch had vanished inside. And by the time the uniformed man had made it to the front door, it was opened by a beautiful, seemingly-ageless woman he knew well.

"Good afternoon, Tommy. Congratulations on your election!"

"Afternoon, Miss Kay; mind if I come in for a spell?"

"Well, I wasn't going to make you sit on the porch! Come on in, and rest your feet for a while."

He followed her in to the beautifully-furnished parlor and accepted the glass of wine she poured him; he had known her long enough to understand that it was best just to accept it because she wouldn't take "no" for an answer. Not that he particularly *wanted* to resist; she made the finest homemade wine in the state.

"I was beginning to wonder when you were going to show your face up here, young man; your father (may he rest in peace) came every week to hear the gossip. He always said I helped him so much that I should have been on the county payroll."

"Well, Miss Kay, that's sort of what I wanted to talk to you about," he said hesitantly.

"Oh?" she asked, refilling his glass.

149

Ladies of the Night

"Well...see, it's like this. Things are different now from when Daddy was sheriff. There's a lot of talk up at the state capital about cleanin' up crime, and about morality and all."

"What's that got to do with me? There hasn't been a major crime in this county since the end of Prohibition, and the rumors we heard helped your father deal with the minor ones."

"Yeah, but what about your operation here?"

"Why, whatever do you mean?"

"Come on, Miss Kay, you ain't dumb. You do a whole lot more'n raise hogs up here."

She laughed. "*That*? Tommy Carson, don't be a fool; nobody in this county cares about that. I bought this house soon after I arrived in this country, and I've been taking in girls and entertaining travelling gentlemen ever since. The people around here know me for a good neighbor."

"Folks around *here*, sure. But like I said, they're startin' to make noise in the capital, and puttin' pressure on local officials like me to clean up."

"Rulers do that from time to time; it's the way of things. They won't know anything about what goes on here unless somebody tells them, and nobody's going to do that."

"Well, maybe. But it's not like it was no more; it's gettin' a lot harder to cover up. An' I'm thinkin' that extra effort has to be worth somethin' to you."

She put down the bottle with barely-controlled anger. "*How dare you*?" she hissed. "Boy, I delivered you, and I gave your mother poultices and medicines for your ailments and rashes and the like. And when she came here sick with worry because you were going off to fight the Germans, who gave her a charm to protect you?"

Pearls Before Swine

Tommy remembered the ancient bronze coin with its faded hawk image and Greek letters; he had worn it on the chain beside his dog tags and though he would not admit it aloud, it had given him great comfort on that beach in Normandy when other men were dying all around him. "And I appreciate all that, Ma'am, I really do. But I figure if a man don't look out for himself, nobody else is like to. You of all people should understand that."

After a long, tense pause her face relaxed, and she poured him another glass. "Of course I do, Tommy. You're right. Things change, and we have to change with them. Let me go over my books, and we'll see what we can arrange."

"I'm glad you decided to see it my way, Miss Kay; I'll come back after the weekend, OK?"

"That'll be fine, Sheriff," she said, seeing him to the door. "Now, mind you drive carefully; that wine is more powerful than you think."

"Now, Miss Kay, it's not your fault."

"Yes it is, Bart, I should never have let him drive; I told him that wine was much more powerful than he thought, but he insisted he could handle it!"

"You know how Tommy is; once he gets a mind to do somethin' neither you nor nobody else is gonna stop him."

"But he could have been killed!"

"Well, he can't be hurt that bad because he was nowhere near the car; after the crash he must've wandered off somewhere to sleep it off. I'm sure he'll turn up; we just figured we'd check here in case he came back to use your phone."

Ladies of the Night

"Please, Bart, let me know as soon as he turns up."

"I'll certainly do that, Ma'am. Oh, by the way, there was a pig wandering around near the wreck; he was real tame so the boys caught him easy and I've got him in the truck. We figured he must be one of yours."

"Yes," she said. "He's one of mine."

(With grateful acknowledgement to Margaret St. Clair).

Pearls Before Swine

Ladies of the Night

"Screening" is the process by which escorts decide whether or not to see a prospective client. Under a criminalization regime like that in the United States, the most important reason for this is to uncover police deceit perpetrated for the purpose of arresting them. But even in the majority of Western countries (where prostitution is legal to one degree or another), screening is conducted to avoid bad or troublesome clients. Some escorts rely heavily on gut feelings or simply ask for referrals, while others have much more rigorous processes. But I daresay nobody else screens quite as thoroughly as Sibyl.

The Screening

Our normal waking consciousness, rational consciousness as we call it, is but one special type of consciousness, whilst all about it, parted from it by the filmiest of screens, there lie potential forms of consciousness entirely different. - William James

    Walter savored the Cohiba and poured himself a second tumbler of Glenfiddich, then turned to look down on the city. Since the year this whiskey went into its cask he had worked to build his business, and after the most recent deal he felt that he had at long last arrived. In all that time he had rarely relaxed, seldom taken a vacation and never allowed himself the luxuries other businessmen did, but all that was about to change; perhaps he might even restrict himself with the kind of business ethics he had always totally disregarded before. But now that he had finally reached the goal he set himself at eighteen, he could afford morality as easily as he could expensive indulgences.

    With that thought, he turned back to his computer screen and hit "send". His days of cheap cigars, second-rate liquor and reasonably-priced escorts were over; now he was playing in the big leagues, and could easily spend the money for a companion of real quality. For him that meant Sibyl, the woman who had fascinated him since he first encountered her website months ago. Still, he had hesitated; though her price was well within his comfort zone, he found her screening requirements rather daunting. He did not like the idea of identifying himself so clearly and definitely to a stranger about whom he knew absolutely nothing, but two

Ladies of the Night

generous servings of Scotch had helped to steel his resolve and now he was committed.

Walter wasn't sure how long Sibyl would take to get back to him, but he certainly didn't expect it to be within minutes. Perhaps it was just an autoreply, though it didn't sound like one:

My Dear Mr. Grey,

Thank you for sending the information I requested! Though I know you've been frightfully busy with that important deal you mentioned in your last letter, I was beginning to think you had perhaps changed your mind about meeting me. I'm glad to see you haven't, and I look forward to meeting you in person after I've finished my screening process, which I'm sure you will understand must be very thorough. I'll let you know by Friday afternoon, but as my preliminary inquiries have indicated that you're exactly the sort of man I like to see, I don't imagine any difficulties.

Very Sincerely Yours,
Sybil

Friday! What kind of damned screening could take three whole days? Walter shrugged, closed the email program, and barely even noticed the fleeting error message which flashed on the screen during the shutdown procedure.

He had thought about taking the next day off, but he was a creature of habit and so eventually found himself at his office again, though several hours later than usual. It was more than early enough; there weren't really very many loose ends to tie up, and he would've been done in plenty of time for a round of golf had he not been required to deal with a long column of annoying emails on a computer which seemed uncharacteristically sluggish, while at the same time dealing with phone calls from the accounting and contract departments. It was a singularly frustrating day, and while it was not bad enough to completely ruin yesterday's celebratory mood, it did demonstrate exactly how much the intense negotiations of the past few months had exhausted him; after his date with Sybil this weekend, a long vacation in the Caymans would be in order. In the meantime, though, a leisurely day tomorrow would help; he had been cooped up in this damned office for so long he kept receiving the bizarre impression that his computer was watching him, and that the screen was its enormous, unblinking eye.

The night's sleep did not alleviate the delusion at all; if anything, the next day was even worse. Every screen he passed or used – his plasma TV, the stereo display in his car, even the touch-screen on his iPhone – seemed to be watching his every move, carefully examining him, peering through his clothes and skin to the nerves, dissecting his brain and smearing his soul onto a slide to be viewed under some impossible, intangible microscope. Walter was far too rational and self-assured to actually believe what he thought he saw; it was perfectly clear to him that this was merely the inevitable but long-delayed result of years of intense stress which would have destroyed a lesser man, but was now catching up to him. Sybil would do him a world of good, and he had already told his secretary he might be out of touch for weeks after he left for his holiday next Tuesday. And though there would be far too many screens at the airport and on the airplane for his liking, he would be far away from the hateful things on a lovely beach in the Caribbean.

In the meantime, though, the scrutiny from the peering eyes behind the screens grew almost unbearable. They watched him from his golf partners' phones after he turned his off, and later from the windows of stores after he covered the car's console screen with his jacket. He felt so surrounded in the restaurant that he was forced to cut his dinner short, and though there was a movie he wanted to see the thought of sitting for over two hours in front of a screen twenty meters wide was absolutely unbearable. So he instead went directly home, took a bottle and glass into his bedroom, and closed the door so he wouldn't have to see the huge flat screen in the living room. He then tried to read for a while, but mostly drank until he sank into terrifying dreams of gigantic, long-lashed eyes prying into every corner of his home.

When he at last awoke to the sound of a ringing telephone, the day was already half gone. The nightmares had finally ceased about dawn, and the beautiful, sultry voice on the other end of the phone heralded a far brighter day than yesterday as Sybil told him that she was done with her screening, and would be happy to see him tomorrow evening as he had requested. She told him the address at which he could pick her up, and suggested they begin the evening with dinner at a restaurant he had heard good things about, but never tried for himself. He hung up the phone with a smile on his face and a much lighter heart, and he dismissed the lingering scent of a strange and spicy perfume as a figment of his imagination brought on by the unsettling presence of the television set within view of his breakfast table.

158

The Screening

Friday afternoon passed without incident, and Walter enjoyed the postponed movie as much as the reviews had assured him he would. A lovely late dinner and a good bottle of wine made for the perfect conclusion to the day, and back at home he laughed at yesterday's ridiculous fears as he flipped channels to relax before bed. His sleep was peaceful and unhaunted by ghastly disembodied eyes, and he awoke the next morning refreshed and optimistic about his date with Sybil and his life in general. He had always regarded his doctor's warnings about overwork with a mixture of amusement and annoyance, but now he recognized that he had been wrong and resolved to apologize at his earliest possible opportunity...after his vacation, that is.

He hurried out for a haircut, had his car washed and went through all the other preparations he would have made for an unpaid date; though he knew Sybil was a professional, he also knew she was very selective and might refuse to see him again if he made a bad impression. He arrived exactly at the agreed-upon time, having already made an electronic payment to her account yesterday as instructed. She was more beautiful than he imagined; her face and body were flawless, her style impeccable and her personality enchanting. The only thing which kept her from total perfection in his eyes was her perfume; it was strange and spicy, yet vaguely familiar and somehow associated with the unpleasant memory of Thursday. But that one sour note soon vanished into the symphony of her presence, and the disquiet it caused was more than drowned out by his rising passion for her.

The next few hours passed in a blur, and Walter felt as excited and nervous as a teenage boy on the drive back.

Ladies of the Night

Her house was nearly as intriguing as she was, and her parlor adorned with all manner of beautiful, unique and obviously expensive furnishings and curios. She offered him a drink, then suggested with a mysterious smile that it was time for her to change…but he felt an unaccountable chill sweep over him when she glided off to a shadowy corner of the room and slipped behind an ornate Oriental screen.

The Screening

Ladies of the Night

The late Ray Bradbury's The Martian Chronicles *first appeared as a series of short stories published in the late 1940s; in the fictional "future history" depicted therein American economic strength and technological prowess grew rapidly in the second half of the century, but society slid into increasing fascism and repression. In this world the '60s brought no civil rights movement, but rather a stifling political correctness that enshrined "rational" thought and resulted in the brutal censorship of imaginative fiction. After the first explorations in 2000, humans descended upon Mars by the thousands from 2001-2005, dotting the red landscape with towns and farms; Bradbury wrote,* "The rockets came like locusts, swarming and settling in blooms of rosy smoke. And from the rockets ran men with hammers in their hands to beat the strange world into a shape that was familiar to the eye..." *Many who came were poor or oppressed, including black Americans in search of a world of their own. But in November of 2005 there was a mass exodus back to Earth in support of a nuclear war, leaving only a few scattered individuals and small settlements behind. Years after* The Martian Chronicles *was published, Robert Heinlein proposed that since the universe is infinite, every world of fiction describes an actual parallel reality. In this story, I imagine an episode from my own life in the world depicted by Bradbury...*

Penelope

"It's time to go."

"I told you, I'm not going."

"Maggie, you can't stay here; the whole town is going. And if you change your mind later, there isn't another rocket within driving distance; most of the others have already left."

"I don't live in town, and you should know by now I don't change my mind once it's made up."

Bill sighed a sigh that came all the way from his shoes, and fidgeted with the brim of the hat in his hands; I watched warily against the possibility of his attempting to physically force me to his truck, and congratulated myself on having had the foresight to place my shotgun within easy reach behind the door.

"Damn it all, woman, if you aren't the stubbornest… what you got worth staying here for? Your husband's already gone."

"Against his will, and even if I went with you I wouldn't be able to see him on Earth. When he eventually gets free, he'll come looking for me here."

"Is that the only reason you're staying?"

"Even if it were, it's Earth that has nothing for me; everything I have I've built here in the last three years. Even my business is illegal there."

"It's not like you're gonna have many customers *here*, either," he spat sarcastically.

"It's not like I'm going to *need* many, with all the bill collectors gone. And even though I won't have any field hands any more, I reckon there's enough food stored in town to keep me alive for decades."

Ladies of the Night

"You could get a different job on Earth; you're the smartest person I ever met."

"What different job? I was trained as a librarian, and that's an obsolete profession in a world where books are banned."

"Not all books are banned!"

"No, only the ones worth reading. I was eight years old when they had the Great Burning, and I've watched the number of banned genres, the penalties for being caught with them, and the powers of the Moral Climate Monitors growing ever since. When I was twenty-eight the burning crew came to destroy the library where I worked after they discovered we were keeping a secret collection, but we were tipped off and had time to hide the books elsewhere. After I came to Mars, I got in touch with the underground and they've smuggled tons of contraband here, where it isn't illegal yet... and never will be if I have anything to say about it."

"You mean you're staying because of a lot of stupid books full of nonsense and fairy tales?" he asked, genuinely incredulous.

"Somebody has to guard our cultural legacy against fanatics, control freaks and the people like you who don't have the spine to stand up to them. Especially if you all incinerate yourselves in an atomic war."

He lunged forward to grapple me, but I anticipated it, grabbed the shotgun and had it leveled at him before he closed half the distance. "You won't shoot me," he scoffed.

"Try me."

With a mix of anger and exasperation he exclaimed, "How long do you think you can wait here alone?"

"Penelope waited twenty years for Odysseus."

"Who are they, more storybook characters?"

164

Penelope

"Something like that," I answered quietly. "Now, please get out of my house."

He crammed his hat back onto his head and stalked out the door, turning at the bottom of the porch steps to yell, "I hope the Martians get you, you crazy whore!" Then he climbed into his pickup and roared off down the drive, leaving a huge cloud of red dust in his wake.

I didn't even wait until he was out of sight, but went for the satchel hidden in my storm cellar, adding a few perishable food items to the things already in it. I made sure my cat and livestock had enough food and water for a few days, shouldered the satchel, picked up the gun and walked out the back door, calling my dogs to follow. By the time Bill returned with a posse to "rescue" me against my will, I had already reached the secret sanctuary I had prepared several weeks ago, when talk of returning to Earth began. I figured they might look as long as 24 hours before giving up, so I made sure I had enough provisions for a week just to be on the safe side.

Apparently, they had enough respect for my competence to recognize that they wouldn't find me if I didn't want to be found, at least not in the available time with the few men they could spare for the search. Early the next morning I was awakened by the sound of thunder, and I watched as the rocket rose swiftly on a pillar of flame, carrying the prodigals back to the world that, in the end, they had never really left. I figured I'd wait until late afternoon to go home, and after breakfast I opened up a volume of Homer to pass the time, mentally preparing myself for what I knew was apt to be a long, lonely vigil.

Ladies of the Night

I'm rather skeptical of the idea that robots will be endowed with anything remotely resembling a human personality anytime within the lifespan of anyone alive at the time of this writing. The reasons for this are complex, though Rachel articulates some of them in this story. For anyone keeping track, this takes place in a little earlier time period than "Rose".

Ghost in the Machine

"Are you sure it's safe?"

"Sure I'm sure. Do you think I want to get sued?"

"I won't be able to sue you if my brain gets burned out."

"It's just a standard psychograph like they've been using for over forty years," Kevin said with more than a hint of annoyance. "You've used one yourself for dubbing sentios."

"Yeah, but you've obviously modified this quite a bit, and a standard psychograph can't do what you've told me this is supposed to do."

He sighed, and made an effort to be patient with her. "You're right, but all I've done is to increase the number and type of receptors and to develop new and dramatically-improved interpretation software. The principle is still the same; it's completely passive, and just records the electromagnetic impulses from your brain. It's a receiver only, not a transmitter."

"OK, OK. I get it. But you can't blame me for being a little scared."

"I don't blame you, Rachel, but you have to believe I wouldn't have signed that contract with you if I wasn't 100% sure this would work. It's a pretty sweet deal for you, after all; half the profit for just a few hours' work."

She leveled a mildly disapproving glance at him. "Really, now. It's my name, my face and my reputation that'll sell this thing, if it sells. And it took me years to earn those."

Ladies of the Night

"I'm not denying that. Let me rephrase it; you've already put in the work, and now you just have to invest a few more hours to cash in."

"*If* it works."

"Why shouldn't it? The principle of recording emotions and feelings isn't new; all I've done is to increase the fidelity and multiply the number of channels so as to take a complete personality pattern. Using that, I can program the simulacrum to act exactly like you, and think of how much guys will pay for their very own Rachel Summers sex doll."

"But that's just it, Kevin; I don't think she *will* act exactly like me. Despite the fact that changes in brain chemistry and physiology can strongly affect personality, we've never been able to locate a 'personality center' in the brain. Lots of psychologists call personality an 'emergent system', something which arises from the neurochemistry of the brain and is contained within it, yet can't be mapped in one-to-one correspondence with it."

"Descartes' 'ghost in the machine', you mean."

"Descartes didn't call it that, a 20th–century philosopher did. Laugh if you want to, but I'm not the only one who believes that the reason true artificial intelligence has never been achieved is that the human brain is qualitatively different from a computer and engineers keep pursuing a quantitative approach."

Though he disagreed with her conclusions, Kevin had to admit Rachel had a first-class mind in that gorgeous head of hers; it was obvious from her sentios, which is why he had approached her with this offer. Lifelike sex robots had been popular for decades, but they had no spirit; they just did as they were told. And while that was infinitely superior to the inert manikins of a century ago, he knew from talk on forums that the first company to produce a doll which could give her

168

Ghost in the Machine

owner what the "hobbyists" of his great-grandfather's day used to call a "GFE", would become rich beyond the dreams of avarice. Programmers had tried to develop an adequate personality simulation for the last decade, but it was no use; nobody had yet developed a robot which could convincingly mimic the personality of an affectionate human woman. So Kevin had hit upon the idea of copying a personality rather than inventing one from scratch, and whose could be better than that of a golden-hearted call girl turned actress, beloved of tens of millions as much for her warmth and humanity as for her looks and sexual skills?

It would work; it had to. "I don't believe in the soul."

She shrugged. "It's your money." Pouring herself into the padded couch, she lifted the helmet to her head and made herself comfortable as Kevin adjusted dozens of settings on the control panel, then signaled he was ready to begin.

Five and a half long, draining hours later, Rachel arose, stretched and announced that she was desperately in need of a steak, a baked potato and a large chocolate milkshake. "How soon will you know if we need to do a retake?"

"About three weeks, I think," he said. "But I'll let you know."

She kissed him on the cheek and said, "I hope I'm wrong." But her eyes said, *I don't think I am.*

Three weeks turned into four, then five; Kevin wanted to make absolutely sure he had everything right. Finally, all the programming was done; it took a few hours to load into the simulacrum, and then he had to wait for agonizing minutes as her systems initialized. Finally, her eyes snapped open, and she abruptly sat up on the table; though she was physically indistinguishable from Rachel, there was something subtly different about her he couldn't quite put his finger on. The doll had been programmed with every aspect of her personality; there shouldn't be anything missing, no behavioral difference between this robot and the real Rachel. And yet she somehow seemed...cold. *Soulless.* He pushed the unwelcome and unscientific thought from his mind and decided to test her responses; if there was a problem he'd discover it soon enough. Better start with the basics, he thought, so he looked directly into the seemingly-human face and said "I'd like a kiss."

Her mouth twisted into a half smile as she looked at him with queenly hauteur and asked dispassionately, "What's in it for me?"

Ghost in the Machine

Ladies of the Night

*Have you ever read any of the old lore about the Fair Folk?
That's the phrase from which the word "fairy" is derived.
They were also called the "Good Neighbors", the "White
People" and similar expressions for the same reason the
Ancient Greeks referred to the horrible Furies as "The
Kindly Ones": it was feared that calling them by titles which
truthfully reflected their reputations might bring down their
capricious and terrible anger. Readers whose only exposure
to the Fay is in the silly, diminutive, insect-winged modern
caricature can really have no notion of how real and
terrifying they were to our ancestors; I prefer to use the
spelling "faerie" so as to make it clear I'm discussing the
beings which inspired Tolkien's Elves rather than something
more closely akin to Tinker Bell.*

Faerie Tale

I met a lady in the meads,
Full beautiful—a faery's child,
Her hair was long, her foot was light,
And her eyes were wild.
- John Keats, "La Belle Dame Sans Merci"

"So, where did you hang her?" Humphrey asked over his pipe.

"I beg your pardon?"

"The portrait, man. The Tudor lady you purchased at the auction yesterday. After what you paid I expected to see her prominently displayed."

"Oh, that." Llewellyn shrugged. "It was a whim."

Humphrey laughed. "I've known you for over twenty-five years and I don't recall your ever indulging such an expensive whim before."

"That's because you didn't know me when I was young; when I first came to London in the sixties I was quite the rakehell."

"I don't believe it; you're the steadiest man I know. Perhaps a few youthful indiscretions, but a roué? Never."

Llewellyn grew quiet for a time and then said, "I tell you that I was the worst scoundrel in the metropolis. I was a bounder and a cad, and if not for the timely intervention of the supernatural I should have ruined the lives of many more women than I did."

There was an uncomfortable pause, which Humphrey eventually broke with, "I have never known you as one to spin yarns, but...see here, Llewellyn, you're a modern man and I know you believe in a rational, ordered universe.

Ladies of the Night

Surely you aren't trying to convince me that you were haunted into reform as Scrooge was."

Llewellyn laughed. "No, not haunted exactly, and to my knowledge I have never seen a ghost. But certainly you would agree that Man has much to learn about the world in which he lives. Ten years ago who would have believed that there existed invisible light rays which could penetrate solid matter and enable a photograph to be taken of the bones inside living flesh? But then Professor Roentgen discovered them, and now they are an established fact."

"In other words, your reclamation was due to some mysterious physical phenomenon not yet understood, yet still susceptible to scientific discovery? I suppose I can accept that."

"Well...not a physical phenomenon exactly. I would say that my reform was effected by some incomprehensible psychical power manifested by a human, or at least apparently human, being."

"Apparently human? I'm afraid I don't understand."

"You're aware that in prehistoric times, there was more than one human species, for example the Neanderthal man. What if one of those races survived into modern times? They might seem outwardly human but be possessed of different abilities and a longer life-span than ours."

"Ah, you refer to the theories of your countryman Machen, that encounters with a near-human species might have given rise to legends of fairies."

"My idea is similar, yes. Many of the old legends surrounding the Good People may thus have a basis in rational fact."

Humphrey smiled. "Am I to believe that you were cured of your dissolute ways by the timely intervention of a fairy godmother?"

Faerie Tale

"Actually, she was a fairy harlot."

"Oh, I say!" Humphrey protested. "This is simply too much!"

"Sit down, George," his friend gently urged. "I shall tell you what happened, and then you can judge for yourself."

"Very well, then," said Humphrey dubiously.

"As you know, my father owned several mills and was quite wealthy by the time I was born; he and my mother both indulged me terribly and never heeded the scriptural advice about the rod. Accordingly, I was quite spoilt by the time I set out for the capital in '62, determined to live my life to the fullest. My allowance was generous and I was skilled at cards, so I had plenty to spend on drink and women, and spend I did. Four years I went on thus, and most certainly would've ended my days with some brother's or father's bullet in my chest had I continued much longer.

"You have probably thought of me as a confirmed bachelor, one of those stony specimens unmoved by the charms of the fair sex, but that was certainly not so in those days; I bedded every woman I could charm or bribe into surrendering her favors, and it concerned me not if she were a professional, a dilettante or a novice so long as she was comely. But over time my appetites grew more difficult to appease, and I began to patronize specialists and expensive courtesans, and to use the more common sort of girl in a most abominable fashion.

"But finally there came to my notice a woman from my own country, herself recently arrived in town; her beauty was said to be incomparable and her skill at singing and playing unsurpassed, and I decided I must have her without delay no matter what her price. My friends warned me not to waste my time; she had spurned every offer she had received, or named prices far beyond their means, but this fixed me all the more firmly in my resolution to enjoy her.

"Accordingly, I made an appointment to meet her and found that the admiration heaped upon her was not exaggerated; she was the loveliest creature I had ever seen, with a voice like an angel, and she sang strange songs in a dialect which was unknown to me and yet hauntingly familiar. And when at last I could wait no longer and pleaded to be allowed her intimate company, the fee she required was quite dear but well within my means.

"That night was like nothing I had ever experienced; I daresay it is not possible to know any greater pleasure this side of the grave. But when I sank, exhausted and unimaginably happy, into a deep slumber beside her, my sleep was disturbed by strange phantasms and I awoke with a vague sense of dread to find myself lying on a floor in an abandoned building. I stumbled into the street in a state of great alarm and confusion, eventually finding my way home hours later and collapsing into my own bed, where I slept until late in the day.

"And since that time, my friend, I have never been able to look upon any mortal woman without comparing her to that peerless nymph and finding her as unappetizing as stale bread. I sank into a deep depression, and only pulled myself from it by devoting my life to scholarship and good works, thus becoming the person you see before you."

Humphrey sat in silence for a very long time before asking, "Do you believe she came to town specifically to turn you from your evil ways?"

"I do believe that, yes. Perhaps she owed some ancestor of mine a favor and resolved to repay the debt by saving me from a wasted life."

Faerie Tale

"Ancestor?"

Llewellyn nodded. He rose and beckoned Humphrey into his study, where the 16th-century painting he had purchased stood on an easel. He then went into a cupboard and withdrew a portfolio containing a number of sketches; they were dated over a period of forty years, and though they demonstrated a gradual improvement in technique over the years they were unquestionably all of the same woman – she of the portrait.

"No mortal artist could possibly do her justice," said Llewellyn with infinite sadness, "but I had no choice but to try or go mad with the need to see her face again. I wonder if the poor devil who painted that" – he gestured toward the antique – "went through the same thing I did."

"Well, the resemblance is certainly striking, but perhaps they're only related," ventured Humphrey, but he knew the falsity of his words even as he spoke them. Even through the imperfect medium of pigment on wood, the subject was enchanting and he found he could not look long into her painted eyes without feeling a strange sense of longing.

Ladies of the Night

Here's another one that I felt belonged in a slightly earlier era. It's based on an idea which was running around in my head since my mid-teens, and which I finally gave form in this story.

The Specialist

Wanda checked her makeup, hair and watch; the client would be there in about 15 minutes. That really wasn't time to do much of anything other than catch up on the news, and though that meant ink on her hands she could wash them quickly enough; one advantage to her clientele was that they tended to be either punctual to a fault, or extremely late. Since the latter circumstances occurred about every fourth date or so, Wanda never scheduled more than one appointment in a given night; she could never get used to the worry when they were late, but the pay was excellent and she really felt she was performing a vital service not merely to her gentlemen, but also to society at large. Besides, she never got tired of their stories.

The newspaper lay untouched and unread on the table as her mind wandered back a few years to that night she had her first special customer; it was a warm night like this one and she had the French doors open so she could enjoy her spectacular view of the skyline. Even on an expensive call girl's income a high-rise penthouse would have been a strain on the budget, but the building's owner was one of her patrons and it amused him to trade rent for services. At first she had been wary that he might demand too much of her per week or attempt to take other unwelcome liberties, but he was very busy and couldn't afford the time even if he had been that sort of man…which as it turned out he wasn't.

It had been a quiet night; her only scheduled appointment had cancelled due to a last-minute change of plans, and since she knew he'd make it good later she was just enjoying a drink on the terrace while listening to her transistor radio. Absolutely nothing could have prepared her for the abrupt appearance of a well-known public figure on a private rooftop forty-five floors above the street, and had she been the panicky type she would surely have screamed. Her immediate reaction was to assume her landlord had finally decided to violate her privacy in order to play out some sort of ridiculous fantasy, but as soon as her visitor started to speak she knew he was the real McCoy.

"I apologize for this unforgivably rude intrusion, Miss Danton, but I'm in need of help and a friend of mine spoke very highly of you."

Wanda was speechless for a moment; "What kind of help could someone like you possibly need from someone like me?"

"The same sort as any other man, Miss. More so, in fact; there aren't many people I can trust, and women..."

"You're wary that women might want to be with you because of your celebrity rather than because of who you are as a person."

He seemed visibly relieved. "Yes, that's it exactly. But I still have the same needs as any other man, and you have a reputation for discretion."

She smiled. "Your visit does me honor, even if your approach is a bit unorthodox. Would you like a drink?"

And that was how it started. After that first night he phoned for appointments like everyone else, always booked multiple hours and paid twice her normal rate so she would leave her calendar clear for the evening just in case he was held up by an "unexpected business meeting." He laughed every time she referred to his delays thus, but he appreciated the fact that she treated their arrangement just that nonchalantly. Inside, Wanda still felt a strange mixture of excitement and fear whenever he arrived for a date, but she never let her face show anything more than the pleasure any

The Specialist

other call girl would show at the arrival of a favored client. Certainly, he could've visited any girl incognito, but he seemed to need to be able to unburden himself about the unusual pressures of his life to someone who would listen without judging and give him simple human tenderness without the expectation of some sort of spectacular performance in return.

It went on that way for the better part of a year, then one night he asked if she minded if he referred her to a friend. "I don't mind at all," she said, "but may I ask if your friend is in the same line of work?"

He smiled. "Yes, he's noticed I was much more relaxed in the past few months and asked the cause. And since he *is* a friend I couldn't very well deny him the opportunity to get to know you as I have."

One referral led to another, and by the time another year had come and gone Wanda had decided to specialize. With rare exception, she had referred all of her regular customers elsewhere and now catered specifically to her exclusive, appreciative and generous "special" clientele. Except for their shared commitment to the cause which united them, they were as different from one another as any other men, so her work never became boring; even their means of payment varied considerably from plain cash to gold or jewels or deposits into her Swiss bank account. Since it was rare that one wished to visit her in the daytime she became a night owl herself and it was not at all unusual that dawn found her just kissing her evening's visitor goodbye. Some were easy to please, some difficult; some were men of few words, and others wanted to talk for hours. But she considered all of them good customers, and wouldn't have

181

wanted to lose a one of them; that was why she worried so when they were late. Though it had never yet happened, she knew it was inevitable that one night an overdue date would never arrive, and then she would have to endure the weary hours until the morning newspaper or news broadcast told her of his fate along with the rest of the city.

It was all worth it; though nobody outside a very select group knew the part she played, that didn't matter one bit. She knew, and they knew, and that was enough. And as that thought crossed her mind, she heard a soft whoosh on her terrace and went out to meet her date, kissing him hello as his powerful arms encircled her and his cape billowed about her in the evening breeze.

The Specialist

Ladies of the Night

Once in a while, an essay or story starts with the title; this is one such case. It was inspired by the Ozzy Osbourne song of the same name, though in this case it has a completely different meaning from that of the song.

The Other Side

The eye sees not itself but by reflection.
- William Shakespeare, *Julius Caesar* (I,ii)

I've been thinking a great deal about reflections of late. Not just in the literal sense, but also in a figurative one; I mean, we all spend so much of our lives *reacting* to things, don't we? One action or situation causes something else to react to it, to reflect from it as a beam of light reflects from a mirror. Take my mum, for instance; had she not been born in a Victorian bordello, would she have become such an awful prude? And had she been less tightly-wound, would I have been so loose? She was like a left-handed reflection of my grandmother, and I in turn a reverse-image of her. Granny's actions made her a wealthy woman, and my mum's aversion to using what she considered a tainted legacy inadvertently preserved it all for my sister and I; then I in turn was shaped in part by not ever having to worry about money. Each generation reflecting from the one before it, endlessly into the past and future, like the row of images one sees when one faces two mirrors toward one another…an endless corridor stretching out in either direction, forever.

Near the end of the Twenties Granny decided she was too old for that sort of thing, and really couldn't keep up any more. The place had declined quite a bit since its heyday in the Mauve Decade, but it was still very lucrative and could no doubt have supported Mum in fine style. But she would have none of it; though she had followed Granny into the business as expected, she never really embraced it, and as my sister Julia reached school age Mum began to fret about the effect of bringing her up in "that kind" of environment

185

Ladies of the Night

(meaning the same one she had been brought up in; my mother was not the most logical of women). She and Granny had a terrible row, and she stormed out with Julia; they didn't speak again for several years. Granny sold the business, bought a lovely little place in a small village in Lincolnshire and retired to go bird-watching and fuss with roses. Mum opened a millinery shop, eventually married and was blessed with her only legitimate offspring (meaning me) in '36. Undoubtedly she intended that I would never meet my grandmother, but Hitler had other plans; when it came time to evacuate us things were hastily patched up, I was given into the custody of Julia (who was seventeen then), and the two of us were bundled out to the country for the duration.

Looking back on it now, I can't remember thinking of Granny as anything other than an absolutely marvelous old lady who was never too strict about how many biscuits I might have before tea. What I mean is, she seemed much of a muchness with the friends' grandmothers I had known in London, only more attentive to me (as was to be expected). Nor did I sense anything odd about the relations between she and Mum when the latter came up for one of her frequent visits, though I do remember asking Julia why Dad never came up with her, and never receiving a satisfactory answer. Granny passed peacefully in her sleep in November of '44; not long after that Julia (who had long since returned to London) married an American bomber pilot, and after the war they moved to California. Then in '51 Dad (who was ten years older than Mum) succumbed to a heart attack, and that left me alone with an increasingly pious, frustrating and overprotective Mum who seemed to believe that demons were lurking behind every lamp-post and plotting to steal my virtue. I couldn't get out of the house soon enough to suit

The Other Side

me, and I'm a bit ashamed to say that I was less sorry than is proper when she followed Dad via stroke in '63.

So there I was: barely twenty-seven, beautiful and rich; good business sense runs in the family, and my mother's business was so healthy its sale more than tripled the trust fund Granny had established for me twenty years before. Most importantly, I was unencumbered by anything remotely resembling a chaperon. As you might expect I went a bit mad, but only socially: when it came to money, I was just as hard-headed and shrewd as Mum and Granny had been. Though I was willing to spend a bit more on a Highgate townhouse than was strictly prudent, I wasn't about to buy all sorts of new furniture when there was plenty of lovely stuff in storage, much of it things from Granny's brothel that she had been unwilling to lose when she sold it. And one of those items is the reason for my waxing philosophical of late, and for my writing this.

As I said there were many fine pieces, including some genuine antiques. And one of them was a huge mirror, large enough to cover most of the wall of a small chamber. I say "mirror" because that's what it evidently was, though the glass had apparently undergone some curious degeneration which turned it a murky black. An expert pronounced the frame Elizabethan, but of a most peculiar design; he said it was almost unheard-of for one so large and so old to have survived with the glass intact, and offered me a ridiculous sum for it. But I was absolutely in love with it and had no need of more money, and I was sure this must have occupied some parlour in my Granny's old brothel. The fact that it was useless as a looking-glass was immaterial; it was gorgeous and started many a conversation at my frequent parties. And that was even *before* the glass cleared.

It had occupied my wall for several years when the change came. One night, several of us were sitting on the floor dropping acid, when there was suddenly a strange shift in the appearance of the glass, as though one patch of the blackness had been suddenly stripped away and light was coming through from behind it. The rest rapidly cleared, and then I saw the image of two people in the glass...that is, two people who were not among those in the room. I immediately called my friends' attention to it, but the view was gone as suddenly as it had appeared; however, it was now a perfectly normal, utterly clean reflective surface. The next day I put the fleeting glimpse of strange figures down to the action of the psychedelic, but the change in the glass was no hallucination: it now reflected the room as though I had replaced the darkened pane with a new sheet of glass. And that, in fact, is what the antique dealer angrily accused me of when I called to ask him how such a thing could happen; he angrily stormed out and cautioned me against wasting his time again in future.

My friends were not so irate as the expert when I told them what had happened, but were no more willing to believe; everyone insisted I was just trying to create a sense of mystery, or hinted that I had been doing too many drugs or watching too many Hammer films. So I stopped trying to convince anyone, and had almost stopped worrying about it when early one morning, while my guest was still upstairs asleep, I wandered into the room and once again saw the image of people – three of them this time – who were absolutely *not* there with me, despite the fact that I was absolutely sober. And though I use the word "people", it was clear that these were not wholly human; they resembled us in

The Other Side

much the same way as one breed of dog looks like another one: same general features, yet unmistakably different. The vision persisted for only a minute, and by the time I had made up my mind that this was not a figment of my imagination it once again showed only a normal reflection.

The phenomenon repeated itself infrequently and irregularly over the next few years. I was afraid, but not to the point of having it crated up again; after all, they were just images, startling but harmless, and Granny had apparently displayed it for decades without mishap. Furthermore, that was an era of exploration and expanding of consciousness; I was convinced that the images were a psychic manifestation rather than a supernatural one, perhaps an attempt at communication by beings from some other dimensional plane. But the glimpses of that world remained sporadic and wholly unpredictable, and eventually they began to unnerve me so much that I decided to return the glass to the state in which I had found it, stored in a dark crate.

I have not looked upon it in over thirty years now, and to be honest I hadn't even thought about it in over a decade; that may seem strange to you, my dear, but you must remember that it was a very different time in many ways. But in the process of going over my affairs, I saw it listed in my notes and realized I should tell you about it, since you'll be inheriting it soon. I'm almost eighty now, and though modern medicine allowed me to survive the event which killed my mother (and no doubt hers), sooner or later I must succumb. You may decide to write this off as an aberration of your senile old Granny who did far too many drugs in her youth, and perhaps you'd be right to; it may be that it was my imagination after all. But before you decide to display it or

Ladies of the Night

sell it, consider this: What if the appearance of the mirror, whether black or reflective or a window into an alien world, is controlled *from the other side*? And during those long periods when we can't see them...

The Other Side

Ladies of the Night

I am informed by a regular reader who is also a theologian that the epigram was not actually written by Aquinas, but only attributed to him by later writers. Still, it accurately reflects a certain attitude prevalent in the Catholic Church up until the Reformation, an attitude which might well have continued had the latter movement been crushed by a slightly more powerful and militant Church, perhaps in a continuation of the Crusades...

For I Have Sinned

**Prostitution in the towns is like the cesspool in the palace:
take away the cesspool and the palace will become an
unclean and evil-smelling place.**
- St. Thomas Aquinas

On Saturday afternoon Sister Magdalene Theodora
filed quietly into the chapel with all the others of her order,
just as she did every Saturday between Nones and Vespers, to
make her confession. It never took long; after all, even the
weakest member of a cloistered order could find few
opportunities for sin. Theodora presumed that most of the
confessions were like hers usually was: a short recitation of
sinful thoughts, admissions of gossip and revelations of
submitting to unorthodox acts in the performance of their
duties, followed by a short penance of the Act of Contrition
and a few *Ave Marias,* or at most a decade or two of the
rosary. It would take less than an hour altogether, and then
the priest would be off to prepare for the vigil mass at his
own church.

But for some time now, she had held back one serious
sin at each confession, then compounded the offense by
taking communion the next day with that mark still upon her
soul. She had no excuse other than fear; the penance was
entirely at the discretion of the priest, and she had seen the
terrible humiliation which could be meted out for the rare
mortal sin. And since the particular canon law she had
(repeatedly) broken left considerable room for interpretation,
she wanted to be absolutely sure her confessor was
sympathetic. When she first resolved to admit her crime
three months ago, she knew that she could never do so to

anyone but Father Anthony; but he had been there only the week before her decision, and not once after that until today.

Theodora wasn't sure why Father Anthony was so fond of her in comparison with the other Magdalene Sisters, but it was obvious to everyone that he was (and the fact had generated some jealousy and more than a few unkind comments). Perhaps he reminded her of a favorite niece, or a girl he had once courted before entering the priesthood; unlike most he had not pursued that vocation directly after school, but rather turned to it after a distinguished military career in the 29th Crusade. He was, in fact, a highly-decorated flying ace, and Theodora had often thrilled to his stories of aeroplane combat in the Pacific against the ruthless forces of the Emperor of Japan. But even though killing in the service of God is no sin, he was pained by the thought of all the blood he had spilled and resolved to pursue the path of peace, entering the seminary less than a year after the end of the war. Perhaps it was this personal history which made him so kind and merciful; that, in combination with his obvious affection for her, helped to quell her fears about the possible outcome of her confession. Try as she might, she just couldn't believe he would inflict a harsh punishment on her; he was more like a kindly old grandfather than a dreaded disciplinarian as Father Gerald had been.

The memory of the fateful day when she stood disgraced before that other priest suddenly intruded upon her consciousness like the unannounced arrival of the Inquisition, and the smiling visage of the beloved Father Anthony was crowded out by Father Gerald's angry scowl. Though it had been fourteen years since she laid eyes on him, she still remembered every line of his cruel face, and the sound of his oddly high-pitched voice as he pronounced her a corrupting influence on the community. "Jack O'Connor was led astray

For I Have Sinned

by this young Jezebel, and now faces months of penance labor!" he shouted; "There is only one sure way to keep her from tempting other young men into sin, one certain method of turning her wickedness to a constructive end!" Her parents' signatures were a mere formality after that, and she was whisked off to a St. Margaret's asylum in New Amsterdam, over a thousand miles from the only home she had ever known. She wasn't even allowed to see the baby; the kindly nun who ministered to her during labor assured her that it was better that way. Then after a brief convalescence, she was transferred to the convent where she would be trained for a life of indefinite penance in the Order of St. Mary Magdalene.

All things considered, it wasn't such a bad existence; they ate well and did little manual labor, because their vocation required the maintenance of their health and beauty. And though they were reviled by chaste women and often made the butt of vulgar jokes, they heard none of it once they entered the gates of the convent because the censors allowed them only wholesome and uplifting books and films. And as the reverend mother and senior sisters frequently reminded them, they served an important social function by protecting others from the effects of what St. Augustine had called "capricious lusts"; by accepting men's sin into their bodies and then doing penance for it every day of their lives, they played a vital role in cleansing the world of evil.

But there was one aspect of her situation which Theodora found almost unbearable, and it was that which had driven her into the transgression for which she now sought forgiveness. Despite the nuns' assurances that her babies

Ladies of the Night

would go to deserving parents who had been unable to have natural children of their own, she was haunted by the memory of the babies – two more since the first – whose cries she had heard, but whose tiny faces she had never been allowed to look upon. She was obsessed with thoughts of what they might be like now; were they happy? Did their adoptive parents treat them well? Did they know their real mother was a sacred harlot, or had that been kept from them? She knew that it was possible one of her regular patrons might eventually marry her, thus freeing her to have children she could keep; in fact, there were two likely candidates and she might well see the outside world again within the next year. But she also knew that she could not stand to have another child ripped from her, and for a very long time now had taken steps to thwart the will of God in that respect. Though submitting to a patron's urging for unorthodox sex acts was one of the minor sins they all confessed every Saturday, Theodora had for years carefully calculated her times of fertility and taken the lead with men she ministered to during those times; thus she had not only sinned herself, but had also tempted others who had sought her services in order to *avoid* sin.

She was unsure how serious her transgression was, but considering that seduction was the offense which resulted in her commitment to this life in the first place, she wasn't going to take any chances. She had faith that God would forgive her; it was only the judgment of His priests she wasn't too sure about. But she knew Father Anthony wouldn't be overly harsh with her; when her turn arrived she glided into the confessional without hesitation, and though her heart leaped when she heard the little grilled window slide open, her voice did not tremble as she started the ritual: "Bless me, Father, for I have sinned…"

For I Have Sinned

Ladies of the Night

What would it be like if sexual needs were given the same respect as other human needs, and sex work the same respect as the other caring professions?

Necessity

Necessity gives the law and does not itself receive it. -
Publilius Syrus, *Sententiae* (#399)

I could tell right away that he was going to be
difficult. To start with, he had put off the appointment four
times, and the delays were accompanied by silly questions
and "I've never done anything like this before"
sheepishness. Then he turned up twenty minutes late, but I
had anticipated that and had nothing else scheduled until after
dinnertime. Finally the door chime rang, and I practically
had to drag him in to prevent his standing there, hat in hand,
as though he were afraid of me.

"Please, sit down and make yourself comfortable.
Would you like something to drink?"

"Yes, ma'am, if it's not too much trouble."

"No trouble. Is iced tea OK?"

"Sure, that'll be great." Then as I returned and
handed him the glass, "You have a nice place here."

"Thank you, Craig. I've tried to make it as
comfortable as possible."

A slight pause, and then, "Do you play?" gesturing at
the chessboard.

"Not very well, I'm afraid," I laughed. "I'm much
better at backgammon, but the chessboard makes a nicer
display piece and a lot of my gentlemen enjoy playing."

A slight twitch of his left eye; he was wound so tight I
was afraid he'd jump if I touched him, so I didn't. "We can
play if you like."

"Oh, no, I'm not very good either, though I'm
studying a book on technique."

Ladies of the Night

"Books are fine, but there's no substitute for experience," I purred. No good; if he caught the double-entendre he gave no sign. I had my work cut out for me. "The set was a gift from my grandfather; he was a chess master and hoped that a pretty set would interest me in the game."

"It's very nice. You said was, has he passed on?"

"Yes, last year."

"I'm sorry."

"Don't be. He had a rich and full life, and when the end came he faced it bravely and without regrets."

"How does your family feel about what you do?"

I would like to think my face didn't register my shock at such an abrupt transition, but I can't be sure. "Well, you know how it is; one's parents often have plans of their own, and they can't help being disappointed when one goes in a different direction."

"What did they want you to do?"

"My father suggested I go into psychology and my mother agreed, and since the subject intrigued me I complied. But while doing my post-graduate work I become interested in sexology, and my doctoral dissertation was on the role of regular sexual activity in alleviating nervous tension in males with high-stress jobs. After I got my degree I decided to become an applied practitioner rather than a researcher, and here I am. My folks weren't exactly overjoyed with my choice, but they respect it even if they don't understand it. How do your parents feel about your career?"

"Oh, my dad's really proud of me, but my mom, well…"

"Mothers never really like it when their children travel far from home, even if it's for important reasons."

200

Necessity

"Yeah, I guess you're right," he admitted. Then, a bit grudgingly I thought, "You're pretty smart."

"Does that surprise you?" I countered.

"Oh, no, I didn't mean that! It's just, well…"

"You didn't expect brains in a whore."

"I didn't call you a whore!" he exclaimed.

"No, you didn't," I said with the most disarming smile I could manage. "Maybe you should."

"I wasn't raised like that!"

Aha! Now I understood his reluctance, and knew how to deal with it. "Craig, you're very young yet, and very idealistic. And while I hope you hold on to as much of that as you can, there are times when one has to be pragmatic. I freely chose this career because I think what I'm doing is important. And if a lot of other people didn't agree with me, we wouldn't be having this conversation right now."

"I know you're right, and I'm actually really excited about being with you. You're very beautiful-"

"Thank you."

"-and I've fantasized about our appointment for the last week," he admitted. "But at the same time I can't help feeling guilty."

"That's not unusual, honey. Lots of my gentlemen feel guilty, especially at first. But men, especially fit and healthy young officers, have physical needs that must be taken care of if they're going to perform at peak capacity. And since necessity demands that you be separated from your wife for the next three years, I'm here to fill in for her in the meantime."

"I know, but I still feel like I'm cheating on her."

Ladies of the Night

"It's not cheating if she knew about it and agreed to it," I said. "I can bring up a scan of her signed disclosure form if you like."

"You don't have to do that, I know. It just feels weird is all, like she only agreed because she had to."

"Nobody was drafted for this mission; everyone here is a volunteer, including you and me. As in any major undertaking, we all have our parts to play. And for Karen to be able to play her part, she can't be here for you now."

He started a little at the mention of his wife's name, forgetting that I had access to the records of all the men to whom I was assigned. "It doesn't seem very fair to you, though."

"I had a choice, just as we all did, and choices carry consequences. Since star travel induces an irreparable degeneration in the ability of a woman's body to carry a child to term, female colonists need to make the trip in suspended animation so as to slow the decay down to an acceptable level. And that means a few of us need to stay awake to keep you men sane and healthy. Maybe one day they'll lick the problem and future couples can experience the voyage together, but for now this is the best solution we've come up with."

"But that means you can never have children of your own," he said with genuine sympathy.

I took his hand. "That's a consequence I accepted. Besides, if I really want them one day I can always employ a surrogate. Maybe your Karen will volunteer, and then she can help me by temporarily taking my place just as I helped you by temporarily taking hers."

202

Necessity

Ladies of the Night

Though the Professor's obtuseness is slightly exaggerated for humorous effect, I assure you that it's not by very much. And though this story is set during the last major anti-prostitution crusade of a century ago, I can further assure you that the Professor's modern counterparts are every bit as bad.

X Factor

Ignorance is preferable to error; and he is less remote from the truth who believes nothing, than he who believes what is wrong. - Thomas Jefferson

When Professor Higginbotham furrowed his brow and stared into the distance, it invariably meant he was wrestling with some abstruse problem. When he steepled his fingers as well, it meant the problem had resolutely resisted his attempts to conquer it for some time. And when he added quiet huffing noises to the mixture, it meant the problem was winning. On this particular occasion, it seemed likely that some new mannerism would join the others to signal a previously-unprecedented level of frustration.

The problem in question was exactly five feet, two and one-quarter inches tall in stocking feet, admitted to one hundred and ten pounds, was somewhere in the general vicinity of twenty-five years old, had brown hair (tinted red) and hazel eyes, and answered to the name "Bernadette" (though it was not the one her mother had given her at birth). She was quite intelligent, terribly witty and could speak English, French and German; she played the piano creditably well, was a good cook (by her own estimation), knew how to drive an automobile and attended every Chautauqua she could; and was also a Presbyterian, a bibliophile, a birdwatcher and a suffragette.

And a prostitute.

And that last was the nub of Professor Higginbotham's quandary.

The learned man had spent some years in the study of the Great Social Evil, and was recognized as an expert in it;

205

Ladies of the Night

he wrote articles for both scholarly journals and popular magazines, and was often asked to speak to ladies' societies and politicians alike on the subject of white slavery. But the professor was not content to rest upon his laurels; he was determined to prepare the definitive text on the subject so as to assist those arguing for its eradication through progressive legislation. But this had proven more difficult than he had at first imagined: the pimps and madams, no doubt fearful of the light he meant to shine upon their noxious trade, refused to allow him access to their charges without payment; and the fallen women he managed to interview on the street or in jails kept giving him outlandish responses which indicated to him that nothing they said could be trusted.

After several months of fruitless effort Professor Higginbotham was sorely tempted to throw up his hands in despair, when suddenly one fine summer evening Bernadette had approached him in the vestibule of a house of ill repute to which he was once again attempting to gain entrance; she introduced herself, asked what exactly he was trying to accomplish and responded to his exasperated explanation by offering to meet him for tea the following afternoon. Though he was reluctant to be seen in public in the company of a known prostitute, the professor was desperate; he accepted her offer, made sure he arrived at the rendezvous early, patiently explained his course of inquiry and asked if she could answer some questions and introduce him to others in her situation who were willing to do the same. He could barely contain his joy when she answered in the affirmative.

Looking back on it, a small voice in the professor's consciousness expressed the opinion that perhaps it would have been better for all involved if he *had* given up; the voice was quickly suppressed by the other elements of the professor's psyche, but not before his ego had heard it and

X Factor

responded with a disapproving frown. Despite his confusion, it was certainly better that he had more data than before, and he was certain that he could eventually reconcile all of the information he had collected with what was already known about prostitution. After all, a great deal of it was not at all problematic; little he had heard from Negro or Chinese prostitutes contradicted his assumptions, and though only a small number of the white girls would admit to having been forced into their tragic straits, that was easily attributable to the shame he knew they must feel, whether they admitted it or not. And while a few of the women of all groups said things he could not easily fit into the model, that was almost certainly a result of the short and superficial interaction he had with them; longer and more thorough interaction would probably have allowed him to discover the reasons for the seeming contradictions, had the women allowed it.

Unfortunately, that line of reasoning did not hold for Bernadette. His association with her was neither short-lived nor superficial; in fact, she had given him more of her time than he could ever have hoped for, and he had come to know her quite well and to feel a greater affection for her than he would have thought possible. He was quite certain that she was both honest and rational, and yet a great deal of what she told him – both about her own life and those of her fellow prostitutes – made no sense to him *at all*. She denied that coercion was common, averred that venereal diseases were not epidemic among them, and insisted that selling their bodies was for most of them a pragmatic response to the abominably-low wages modern industrial society offered women, rather than the result of coercion, congenital degeneracy or moral turpitude. And even if he could dismiss her claims as beliefs which her sweet nature had constructed in order to protect her mind from the dreadful reality inhabited by her sisters, the fact remained that they were certainly true for her *personally*.

When the anomaly first became apparent, the professor suspected that she was not actually a prostitute at all; he was, however, forced by the evidence of his own senses to abandon this theory in very short order. He then reasoned that her declaration of contentment with her lot was merely a defensive pose which would crumble the moment she saw a way out of her awful condition; however, when she turned down his sincere offer of honorable marriage, it became clearly obvious that she was telling the truth. The contradiction was maddening: Bernadette was an intelligent, sensible, well-bred, well-educated girl without a dishonest bone in her body who claimed not only to have chosen a filthy, degrading trade for rational, practical reasons, but also to be not unusual in that respect. This flew in the face of everything Professor Higginbotham knew; there must be some missing variable, some x factor as it were, which explained why Bernadette and a few others like her could submit to men's bestial desires for money without having been forced to do so by man, nature or bad company. But what that x factor might be had eluded the professor for weeks, and had stubbornly refused to reveal itself to him today despite his devoting the deepest cogitation to it all afternoon.

His level of frustration can be judged by the fact that an impossible solution had presented itself to his searching mind several times already today: what if she was right, and he was wrong? What if her analysis was exactly correct, and the common wisdom about the flesh trade, developed through the work of three generations of dedicated scholars, had

X Factor

veered radically away from reality due to incomplete data and fallacious initial assumptions? What if a certain fraction of women were neither asexual nor as subject to lust as common men, and were thus able to exploit men's desires to earn a living for themselves, just as any entrepreneur might prosper by taking advantage of human frailties? What if harlots were neither victims nor villains nor vixens, but simply businesswomen?

But no, it was preposterous; it would mean the whole citadel of social thought had been constructed on a faulty foundation without anyone having noticed. Such things simply couldn't be true; they were as fanciful as Mr. Wells' scientific romances. No, there must be something else, some credible factor which did not require the re-thinking of everything that was known about womankind.

Perhaps Bernadette was a witch…

Ladies of the Night

Like "Mercy" and "Friend", this story was inspired by an existing fictional character; unlike the others, this character still appears in a contemporary format, so I suppose this story could be loosely classified as "fan fiction". I think the story stands well on its own, so I won't mention who the beloved is; however, if you can't work it out from the clues and your curiosity demands an answer, take a look at the comment thread for my blog of February 13th, 2012.

Companion

I don't know how to take this.
I don't see why he moves me.
He's a man. He's just a man.
And I've had so many men before,
In very many ways,
He's just one more.
- Tim Rice, "I Don't Know How To Love Him"

Deep down, I always knew this day was coming, but I simply didn't want to believe it; like any other woman, I desperately clung to the belief that I was somehow different, that I was the one you would never leave. Or failing that, at least that it wouldn't hurt so much when you eventually said goodbye.

When we met, I was so sure of my self-control, so confident of my resistance to male sweet-talk. I thought I had heard it all, learned how to deflect every line, every strategy, every silver-tongued attempt to circumvent my barriers to get some special deal. But you outmanoeuvered me at every turn. I guess it isn't surprising, considering that you had already racked up a long tally of broken hearts before I was even born, but I didn't know that then; I couldn't imagine how completely outclassed I was until it was far too late.

But the bait was so tempting, the deal so apparently straightforward: "Come travel with me," you said; "I'll pay you all you ask and more, and you'll see and do things few other women have ever seen and done." Coming from anyone else that would've been an obvious lure, but you managed to make it sound so convincing – especially

Ladies of the Night

considering what I had already learned about you in our first
chance encounter. I'm not saying it was a lie; you were as
good as your word. You've showered me with money and
gifts, so generously that if I invest wisely I'll never have to
work again. And if anyone else has *ever* done some of the
things we've done together, I've never heard of it. I've seen
wonders I could only have dreamed of, walked in places I
never knew existed, and experienced feelings ranging from
near-bliss to mortal terror. I'll certainly have no dearth of
stories to tell my grandchildren, though I doubt they'll
believe me.

Of course, you weren't really travelling all those
places for me; you were going anyway, and just wanted some
company on the journey. And wealth comes so easily to you;
pick up a few things cheap in places where they're common,
sell them dear in places they're rare or unique, and before
you know it you're as rich as Croesus with less effort than it
takes to decide what you want for tea. Everything comes to
you like that – travel, money, women – and because it does
you don't truly value any of it. Money becomes merely a
means to your ends, one place is a great deal like another and
women are as replaceable as any other creature comfort.

Don't say I'm being unfair; yes, I know, you love
everybody. But don't you see, loving everybody is the same
as loving nobody? When love is just a principle rather than a
feeling, it loses all personal meaning; I'm sure you want
"justice" for me as well, but that will hardly be a comfort
during all the long, lonely nights to come.

Have you picked her out yet, my replacement I
mean? I can think of a few likely candidates; I've seen the
way you looked at some of the women we've encountered of
late. And I know you have a knack for "accidentally"
running into someone again when you want to, even though

Companion

you and I both know that with the way you travel, the odds against such a second meeting occurring purely by coincidence are completely astronomical. It's just one more example of the way you fix the game to get the outcome you want.

Please, don't look at me like that, and don't act as though I'm really hurting your feelings; I'm sure that I'm not the first woman to react in this fashion. You probably can't even count the number of similar scenes you've played, much less remember the names of the actresses. And now it's my turn; "Exit, stage left". My goodies are all packed, and I see we've arrived at the home I left all those many months ago (or is it years? It's been so hard to keep track). All that remains now is for me to walk out that door with my valises, then turn around and watch you quite literally vanish from my life forever, off on new adventures with a new companion.

Ladies of the Night

Every principled person encounters the occasional ethical dilemma, and most of us have urges and desires which sometimes conflict with our principles. But I truly hope none of your dilemmas are as knotty, and none of your conflicts as violent, as those with which Gloria has to contend.

Monopoly

It is small wonder that people find "free choice" a confusing idea: [it] appears to refer to what the person being judged...does, whereas it is actually what the person making the judgment...thinks. - Thomas Szasz

I will never understand why people feel compelled to stick their noses into others' business. Everyone is different, and has different needs and desires; we also each have different strengths and gifts. If one person has something another wants, and that other has something the first wants, and they agree to a trade, how is that anyone else's concern? If you've got money and want food, and a grocer or restaurateur has food and wants money, and the two of you agree to an exchange, that's business; both parties go away happy. And if one of you is dissatisfied with the transaction – say you thought the quality of the food was poor or the service was lousy, you simply don't go back; you instead find another food vendor who will give you what you demand for your money. That's competition, and it's what keeps the free market free. Some ridiculous people want to claim that it's somehow exploitative to sell people things they want, and some even *more* ridiculous people claim it's exploitative to offer to pay someone for something. These people are living in a fantasy world; here on the material plane, there is nobody who doesn't need or want *something*, and very few who have absolutely nothing to offer in exchange. As long as the transaction is voluntary, nobody else has the right to say boo. It's only when someone is actually coercing the other that there is an issue.

Ladies of the Night

"But Gloria," you ask, "what if one party's need for whatever the other one has is so strong it constitutes coercion in and of itself? What if the customer is addicted to the product, or the seller is so poor he's desperate for money?" Well, what of it? You're probably addicted to caffeine, so does that mean Starbucks is exploiting you when you walk in for one of their overpriced lattes? You could just as easily go to McDonald's. As long as there's a free market, you can still choose who's going to get the money you spend on your caffeine addiction. The same goes for food, medicine, shelter and everything else. And yes, even labor; if one company offers poor wages and another fair ones, who is everyone going to apply to? It's only when there is no real competition because there's a monopoly or a cartel, or because a coercive government fixes prices or establishes a restrictive licensing regime or the like, that exploitation arises because the one who needs the artificially-limited thing is at the mercy of whoever can provide it.

And that is the crux of my ethical dilemma.

In my youth I developed a strong sense of morality and fair play, and despite considerable pressure to abandon it I have never compromised. But now I find myself in the uncomfortable position of having a local monopoly on the service I provide, and I'm extremely concerned that I might begin maltreating my clients because of it. I've even toyed with the idea of initiating another lady so that I'll have a competitor, but the only problem with that is I couldn't be sure she would maintain my high ethical standards. See, the service I sell is…well, kind of addictive I suppose. Once a man has experienced my…attentions, he tends to want them again and again; the temptation to take advantage is therefore very, very high, and I think it's very likely that any self-created competition would not be as resolute as I am. In

216

Monopoly

other words, in trying to avoid exploiting my clients, I would almost certainly expose them to greater exploitation.

As you've probably guessed, I'm a Lady of the Evening. Yes, I know that term sounds so old-fashioned nowadays, but "prostitute" is so legalistic, "sex worker" so vague and most of the other choices so vulgar…and I sincerely doubt most Americans would even know what "demimondaine" meant. And yes, of course there are plenty of others around; there are probably hundreds of women of every type and stratum within an hour's drive, all easily contacted via email. But I offer a very unusual service, catering to a kink that used to be relatively rare but is now increasingly popular. See, in the past I could count on that rarity to keep me honest; so few men were interested in what I was selling that I had to carefully cultivate each one lest I "kill the golden goose" as it were, and be caught with fewer clients than needed to maintain my preferred lifestyle. But now, I could treat my clients like dirt were I so inclined, drain each one dry and then discard him, secure in the knowledge that there would be plenty more where he came from. And that's not only wrong, it's dangerous; in my line, one has to avoid attracting undue attention.

Ah, well, I didn't really expect you to have a solution; I mean, it's not like you've ever been in my position, now is it? But sometimes, it just helps to talk to somebody, to voice these things out loud instead of merely letting them rattle around in my brain. Thanks for listening; how much do I owe you? Maybe we'll talk more another time; I really must fly now. I have to meet a gentleman at eleven, and it's after ten now; I haven't far to go, but it takes a lot longer to make sure one looks nice when one can't make use of a mirror.

Ladies of the Night

In contemporary Western societies, governments attempt to control prostitution because it is stigmatized as "dirty", "bad" or "wrong". But it was not always so; in many ancient cultures the harlot was a kind of priestess, a gateway through which men might experience the Divine Feminine. Indeed, there are still some traditions in which the act of selling sex is considered sacred, and there is no reason to believe that could not become the dominant view again, given the right social conditions.

Vocation

Badness you can get easily, in quantity; the road is smooth, and it lies close by. But in front of excellence the immortal gods have put sweat, and long and steep is the way to it. - Hesiod

      Maru had been done with her packing for hours. Not that there was all that much to do; the few meager belongings she could call hers had been tied up in a cloak, and she had donned her ornaments and her good gown. Soon she would leave for the assembly, and when it was over she would bid her friends and family goodbye and accompany the priestess back to the temple.

The narrow dirt streets of the village were thronged with girls and women eager to hear the priestess speak. Once per month (on the sixth day after the full moon), a priest or priestess would arrive to address the people; everyone would gather in the square to hear the latest news from other parts of the kingdom, to ask questions and present grievances to be taken to the Priest-King, and to listen to the sermon. An acolyte also accepted letters to be delivered to other parts of the realm, and handed out any letters from elsewhere. After dinner would come a talk about vocations, and those youths or maids who wished to return to the capital to be trained for one of the available positions would come forward to give their names, and early next morning would join the priestly entourage on its journey to the next village.

      The first and second months of spring were slightly different, though. Last month the priest of the war-god had come, resplendent in his magnificent armor, to speak only to the men and boys; as usual, several of the youths who had

219

Ladies of the Night

reached manhood in the past year had departed with him to be trained as priests, warriors or (in cases of unusual ability) both. And this month it was the priestess of the love-goddess, whose meeting was open only to women and girls; Maru had decided several years ago that once she became a woman, she would follow the call to become a temple harlot. She was widely recognized as the most beautiful maid in the village, and her natural grace and clever mind had long been remarked upon. More than anything else she wanted an education and a chance to serve her people by caring for the needs of the great men in the service of the Priest-King, and the old women of the village were all certain she would be accepted.

But as she listened to the priestess, Maru began to doubt. The holy woman was the epitome of poise and grace; her clothes were magnificent and her hair beautifully arranged, and if she had ever spoken in some provincial dialect there was no trace of it now in her perfect elocution. She was everything Maru could ever wish to be, but she feared it was hopeless; still, she had come this far, and had to try. All through the long afternoon she worked to reassure herself, but had no appetite at dinner and began to worry that her voice would fail when it came time to speak.

At last, the moment arrived; the call for vocations had been given. Maru felt herself stand and heard her own voice speak her name, but it was almost as if someone else had accomplished it for her. She felt every eye upon her, but the tension was broken in an instant when the priestess smiled and said, "I'm so glad you're joining us, Maru; I've had my eye on you for two years now, and I'm sure the goddess is as pleased as I am." A great shout broke out among her friends and kin, and she felt she would be suffocated by hugs and kisses.

220

Vocation

When she met the priestess in the square at dawn she was given a novice's gown of plain white linen, and on the journey to the next village some seven hours away the great lady braided her hair and spoke to her as if they were peers, answering every question Maru could think of and listening while the girl told her more about the village and its people than she could possibly want to know. The acolyte, Zuza, was only about two years older than Maru; she was as friendly as her mistress, and by the time they arrived at their destination Maru felt as though they had been friends for a long time. Her heart swelled with pride as she saw the way the village girls looked at her, but she followed Zuza's example and carried herself humbly, as a servant of the priestess.

They travelled thus from town to town for three weeks, and were joined on the way by three more girls; one aspired to the priestesshood, another wished to learn the healing arts and the third was an orphan whom the priestess had accepted as a servant of the temple; had even one more joined their number someone would have had to ride up front with the driver. At last the tour was over, and on the day of the next full moon they arrived at the city which served as the capital of this province; from here they would depart for the City of the Gods, where the Priest-King ruled and all the great temples stood. Maru's father had been to the provincial capital once, years before she was born; but none of her family had ever been to the Royal Seat, which lay so far to the east it would take months to get there even on a fast horse.

But there were no longer any roads upon which to make such a journey; the great thoroughfares crossing the

Ladies of the Night

wastelands had fallen into ruin since the end of the Golden
Age, and the only practical means of travel across the
wilderness was the one they would board in the morning.
Though Maru had heard them described and even seen
pictures, nothing could prepare her for the awesome sight of
the airship, longer than the main street of her village,
gleaming like burnished brass in the last rays of the setting
sun.

Vocation

Ladies of the Night

Though the stories which appear in my blog most months vary in tone as you have seen, those I publish in December are always light and upbeat. This doesn't mean they have nothing to say, but rather that they say it with a smile and perhaps a wink. Like "Pandora", this story was based on a dream. But perhaps because it was a cute one rather than a terrifying one, I turned it into a tale right away rather than waiting several decades.

Visions of Sugarplums

They err who thinks Santa Claus comes down through the chimney; he really enters through the heart.
– Mrs. Paul M. Ell

It all started when I got a call from my very best client, offering me several days at one of the most beautiful resorts in known space, during which he'd be busy every daylight hour and most of the evening; all I had to do is look beautiful, be incredibly charming at dinner, make sure his suits were perfect and laid out before bedtime, give him massages when necessary, spend 15 minutes on my back most nights, collect my pay and be home in time for Christmas. Best of all, it was his wife's idea; she despises space travel and would rather delegate consort duties whenever her husband goes offworld. All in all, just about the nicest, cushiest booking imaginable. And it did turn out okay in the end, but...

Hang on, I'm getting ahead of myself. The trip out was uneventful, and these new diplomatic ships are so damned fast we arrived at Alinor in only three days. And that's when I got my first unpleasant surprise; like a complete dorp I had forgotten that Alinor is a whole planet, and though there are indeed lots of gorgeous resorts in the temperate zone, we were in the tropics. And not Hawaii or Tahiti-type tropics either, oh no; we're talking thirty-five degrees in the shade, eighty percent humidity tropics. See, the Tsath – those are the aliens my client was there to negotiate with – are rather like enormous frogs, and cool, dry air can make them sick.

Ladies of the Night

But I'm nothing if not professional, so I smiled and resolved to make the best of it. "Just be friendly," he said; "you're certainly good at that. Think of yourself as a goodwill ambassador."

"What, to the Tsath? Do they speak English?"

"Remarkably well. They're linguistic prodigies; the consul herself speaks at least eleven that I know of. But their thinking is emotive and subjective; they rely on intuition over logic and prefer art to science, so we're trying to work out a deal to provide them with technicians and automated factories. Just between you and me, they're really very backward."

"Is that why you in particular were sent here?"

"Yes. We've been trying to finalize this deal for months, but though the Tsath are clearly eager to trade with us, we just can't seem to come to an understanding. It's as though they were waiting for something."

"Well, maybe they are. You said they were intuitive and backward; maybe they're waiting for an omen or an auspicious conjunction."

He looked at me as though I had said something he hadn't thought of before and said, "Maybe they are, at that."

One of the locals had told me about clothes of a fabric designed to draw heat and perspiration away from the skin, which made the climate quite bearable; so, I decided to make an early start on the second day and go out into town to buy an outfit or seven, but as I was crossing the lobby I suddenly found myself face-to-face with the Tsath negotiator.

"Good morning, Miss Kane! You are just the person I wanted to see!" Her English was absolutely flawless, but what really amazed me was that she could tell humans apart

Visions of Sugarplums

so easily; she had only seen me once, at last night's dinner, and to me she was nearly indistinguishable from the others of her party but for her insignia of rank.

I bowed my head and closed my eyes for a moment in the Tsath gesture of respect, then said, "You do me honor, Madame Consul; what can I do for you?"

"When I asked Mr. Ituro if you were his wife, he explained that you were a paid companion. Is that correct?"

I inwardly panicked for just a moment; if these people were backward, might they have a primitive prejudice against whores? But her voice sounded pleasant and friendly; I decided honesty was the best policy. "Yes, it is."

"Ah, I didn't know Earth people had the trade, too! Well, if you don't mind, I have a contract for you."

Before I could think of a reply, she called out to someone, and a Tsath child emerged from behind a display she had apparently been reading. She was cute, in a 30-kilogram-deep-purple-tree-frog-with-spindly-limbs kind of way; fortunately for me, though the Tsath had no visible sexual dimorphism my unschooled eyes could discern, their customs of dress were coincidentally like traditional Western ones: one could tell a girl by her skirts.

"How fortunate I am to have found someone who could keep Nahgi company while I am embroiled in negotiations! Whatever price you ask will be fine with me; you have an honest face so I know you'll be fair."

"I'm, uh, very pleased to meet you, Nahgi," I stammered, totally unsure how to handle this.

"I'm pleased to meet you too, Miss Kane," she squeaked in perfect English. "I just know we're going to have ever so much fun!"

Ladies of the Night

"I'm sure we will," I agreed, feeling very trapped as I watched her mother vanish into the lift.

Though it was rough going at first, I eventually realized she wasn't all that different from a human seven-year-old, and though I hadn't baby-sat since I was sixteen it came back quickly enough. I got to see their intellectual dimorphism firsthand: though technical things seemed to confuse or fascinate Nahgi far more than they would a human child, her facility with languages was quite remarkable. She spoke three in all, and despite the fact that she had never heard English at this time last year, she now sounded like a native. I soon realized that she found endless amusement in puns, rhymes and silly word games, though not nearly as much as she found in my painfully-incompetent attempts to pronounce even the simplest words in her language. She was very excited by my promise to teach her a bit of Mandarin the next day, yet at the same time was mystified by my ability to add up the prices of items in my head.

And so, in spite of my initial reluctance, I actually found myself enjoying the day. The marketplace was climate-controlled for human comfort, so I had bought her a little winter suit to keep her warm; she laughed at herself in the mirror and I laughed to see the contrast of my pale human skin in summer clothes with her hairless purple head sticking up from a faux-fur collar. Fortunately, she had been taught which human foods she could eat, but when I took her to the penny arcade after lunch I found that most of the games either bored or frustrated her. Since I was feeling generous and growing genuinely fond of my little charge, I suggested she show me the sorts of playthings she liked in the toy

Visions of Sugarplums

department; this was met with the same enthusiasm one
would expect from a human child, so off we went.

When we arrived, I thought her already-huge eyes
would bug completely out of her head. The proprietors of the
shop had decorated it for the holidays in the antique style of
centuries past, with old-fashioned garlands and colored
lights; dolls and toy animals ran about the floor, and aircraft
flew in formation or performed aerobatics. A wide selection
of Christmas music from many different times wafted
through the air, as did the savory smell of baked goodies
presented on trays for the taking. Artificially-created snow
was falling in an enclosed playground out front, and colonial
children who had never seen the stuff except in video romped
and howled, building snowmen and pelting each other with
snowballs. And presiding over the whole from his throne at
the back of the area was Father Christmas himself, in the
same costume he's worn since before children first
accompanied their parents to the stars.

"Who is *that*?" Nahgi asked in a hushed voice.

"He's dressed as a legendary figure called Santa
Claus, who is the symbol of our most popular festival. That's
what all these decorations are for."

"Is Santa Claus a god?"

My stomach dropped. I had no idea what Tsath
religious beliefs were like, though her question seemed to
indicate polytheism. On the one hand, I might start an
interstellar incident by insulting their faith, but on the other
hand, I wasn't about to tell a child of any species that Santa
wasn't real. So I opted for the diplomatic approach.

"Well, a saint. Sort of a demigod, I guess; I'm not an
expert in theology." Oh, good grief; what an inane answer!

Ladies of the Night

As soon as it was out of my mouth I wanted to drown myself in the wassail bowl.

But Nahgi didn't think it was stupid, at all. "So, this is a priest dressed as him for a ceremony!"

"Something like that."

"Why are the children setting on his lap? Is he blessing them?"

"Well, sort of. They tell him what gift they would like, and the legend says that if they've been good, he brings it to them on Christmas Eve, which is six days from today." She was so excited I thought she would wet herself, if Tsath do that. "May I sit on his lap, too?"

For a moment, all I could see was a vision of myself standing neck-deep in a hole, which I was digging deeper and deeper. "Well, I would suspect so, but let me ask permission first, OK?" She gave that closed-eye nod, and I approached Santa to ask; as it turned out he was a retired xenobiologist and was absolutely thrilled to share the ancient ritual with an alien child. I beckoned her to the throne, and though she at first approached with awe she was as quick as any human child to clamber into his lap once he bade her do so. And as I watched the timeless scene unfold for a little girl to whom it was wholly new, I thanked the goddess of my profession for tear-proof makeup.

Once she had whispered her Christmas wish to him, hugged him and climbed down, she scampered gaily to my side and took my hand. "I'm ready to go back to the hotel now, if you are," she said.

"What did you ask him for?" I asked, my heart in my fallen stomach.

"For our people to reach an agreement soon," she said.

230

Visions of Sugarplums

I felt a pall of doom descend upon me. "Sweetie, I'm not sure he can bring you that."

"Yes, he can," she said matter-of-factly.

She was right.

By dinner the next day, the talks were concluded; the Tsath had clearly received whatever omen they had been waiting for, and the agreement had fallen into place as quickly and neatly as one might negotiate the sale of a used robot. My patron was mystified; he had no idea what had happened, but being male he was satisfied with the assumption that his own skill at negotiation had somehow broken the impasse. The consul thanked me at dinner for taking such good care of Nahgi, and the child herself came to see me the next morning, to hug me goodbye and to ask for my address so she could write; neither of them said anything about the resolution, either.

I'll tell you what I think happened, though. The Tsath are creatures of intuition; the negotiators probably projected the typical human "serious grown-up business" demeanor, which may have made them uncomfortable and wary. But when I spent a day with one of their children, and allowed her to see that Earth people were capable of generosity, humor and tenderness, it forged a connection that wasn't there before. Maybe the Tsath have a kind of Santa Claus, and the discovery that we do as well showed them our two peoples aren't so different after all.

(*With grateful acknowledgement to Zenna Henderson*).

Ladies of the Night

Like the first story in this collection, the last one is both longer than usual and took shape outside of the constraints of my blog. It was, in fact, written specifically for this collection, and based on an idea woven from many different threads of folklore, fiction and fancy sometime in my early twenties, which I had never turned into an actual story before now. It's an exploration of several things all too many modern people seem to have either forgotten or willfully denied: the glory and pain of risk; the recognition that life is ultimately a solitary journey; and the uncomfortable fact that the laws of biology were not designed with human happiness in mind.

Nephil

That the sons of God saw the daughters of men that they were fair; and they took them wives of all which they chose. - Genesis 6:2

"Tell me about my father." I had heard that often over the years, but it had changed; the question came more often now, and he seemed to be in search of specific information rather than the things I had already repeated countless times since he was first old enough to ask.

"You already know everything I know, Jason. I'm not sure what else I can tell you."

There was a long pause, and then: "Was there anything...unusual about him?"

Well, that was different. "He was unusually good-looking."

"Mom, please."

I feigned a lightheartedness I did not feel. "Well, it's true! I'm sure you've noticed I don't date just any old man! I have high standards."

"Too high to sleep with a man just because he's attractive."

I had always been honest with him about sex, but one still doesn't expect that sort of reply from one's sixteen-year-old son. "There's no need to be rude."

"Not rude, honest. Just like you always are with me."

Touché. "I was a lot younger then."

"Aunt Becky says you were always picky, even in high school."

"Jason, I'm sure you've noticed by now that you don't always know why you find one girl more attractive

233

than another, and that's doubly so for women. Your father was older and much more experienced than I was; he was intelligent and witty and had a powerful magnetism that would have made him difficult to resist even if I had wanted to. And I didn't want to."

"You're always lecturing me about using protection; why didn't you?"

"Oh, now this is too much!"

"It's a fair question, Mom. You weren't foolish, even when you were eighteen; everybody says that. So I can't believe you let some guy, no matter how smooth, talk you into unprotected sex."

"Sweetie, it was a different time. AIDS was still a few years in the future, and we hadn't had the Gospel of Condoms drilled into our heads yet. It was much easier then to convince oneself that if a guy looked clean, he was."

"But there was still the chance of pregnancy! Why did you risk that?"

"I didn't think I was risking anything; I just miscounted."

"I find that hard to believe."

"You are the proof," I said aloud. But the truth is, I hadn't; I was extremely regular, and had finished my period only the day before my first and only sexual encounter with his father. But like an example out of an abstinence-based "sex education" lesson, I had become pregnant anyhow.

It was the summer of 1981, and I was invulnerable. I had a full scholarship and a small legacy from my late great-grandmother; it wasn't much, mind you, but it was enough for a frugal girl with two roommates who wasn't afraid to get around by bicycle. It was still over a month before school

234

Nephil

started, but my friends and I had all been anxious to get out from under our mothers' watchful eyes and spread our wings a bit. And boy, did we ever; Theresa's parents had more money than sense and had given her a brand-new Mercedes, a generous allowance and a credit card for "emergencies", and so she decided the three of us would go touring for a few weeks, her treat. She let us know that this was only a one-time thing, and that once school started we would have to contribute equally; but for now, we were celebrating, and Theresa was not inclined to be parsimonious.

For three glorious weeks we wandered hither and yon, wherever the road would take us; when we got tired we would stay in a four-star hotel where one was available, and in whatever *was* available when luxury wasn't. We lay on beaches, went to shows, gambled in Las Vegas and even visited Yosemite National Park; we ate at gourmet restaurants and hot-dog stands, drank champagne and smoked weed, and otherwise behaved in a carefree and wholly irresponsible manner. Theresa and Jill both went off with guys on a couple of occasions, but nothing we encountered had struck my fancy until I met Jim.

We were staying at some crappy little hotel in a reasonable approximation of the middle of nowhere. The car had started to run hot and Theresa, though extravagant, was not foolish; we stopped in the next town, found a garage and were told the new water pump wouldn't be there until the next day. My friends used the opportunity to get good and smashed, but I just wasn't in the mood; they were out cold before ten, so I decided to go for a moonlight swim in the hotel pool, which was just about the nicest part of the place.

Ladies of the Night

"Would it bother you if I joined you?" His voice startled me; I hadn't heard him approach.

"No, not at all," I said, still believing myself invulnerable. And it didn't hurt that he was a strikingly fine-looking specimen. He had excellent manners, too; he entered at the opposite end of the pool and made no attempt to approach me, but instead swam back and forth along the edge of the pool, leaving the rest of it to me. But being in a strange place, far from anyone who might judge, sometimes emboldens a girl; it certainly did me. "You needn't stay so far away, you know; I'm not radioactive or anything."

He slipped under the surface, kicked off from the side and had surfaced near me in less time than it takes to tell; he swam with the speed and grace of a sea lion. "Are you sure I'm not bothering you?" he asked.

"I'm sure." Now that he was this close, I realized that I had underestimated his looks; I am not exaggerating when I say that he was the most attractive man I have ever met, either before or since. It wasn't just his splendid physique, his handsome face or his gorgeous eyes; it was a kind of presence, a raw appeal unlike anything else I've ever felt. But I am considered quite a beauty myself, and that was even more true seventeen years ago; nor was I ever prone to attacks of false modesty. I was very used to being "hit on" by men, and had the self-confidence necessary to hold my own even in the presence of an Adonis. "So, what in the world are you doing in this place?"

He laughed. "The same thing as you, I imagine. Sometimes the realities of life force us to interrupt our travels momentarily. Pleased to meet you; I'm Jim."

"Ha, my brother's named Jim. I'm Michelle."

And that was how it started. I don't remember the exact details of the conversation, but I do remember that I

236

was the one who did most of the talking; Jim was sweet and well-spoken, but every time I tried to turn the conversation to him he effortlessly guided it back to me in short order. When I thought back on it later I realized that he had told me almost nothing about himself, and what he did tell could've been about almost any man. At the time, however, I barely noticed; he seemed to know exactly what questions would set me to talking about myself or some subject I was interested in, and asked them whenever necessary to keep me going. We talked on the side of the pool for over three hours, then we moved on to doing more than talking, and then he got a room for us. And it wasn't until I woke up alone the next morning that it struck me as odd that he hadn't already checked in before coming to the pool.

"OK, let me ask it a different way; am I a lot like my father?"

"You know you aren't. You took after my side exclusively; why, you're the spitting image of your Uncle Jim."

"Maybe, but I'm not anything like him in personality. And not much like you, either."

"A geneticist's son should know better. Though some personality traits do seem to be inherited, others are clearly the result of nurture over nature, and still others are a mystery."

"Yet you yourself have written several papers on the genetic basis of behavior."

"Instincts are not the same as personality."

237

Ladies of the Night

"They can be. Cats still act like cats even if they're taken from their mothers at a young age."

"Yes, but those traits are the same across *all* cats. Those aspects of their personalities which differ between individual cats aren't heritable."

"Still, some really complex behaviors can be transmitted through the genes."

"Well, sure; web-building and salmon spawning behavior, for example. And clearly, a lot of human behavior is the product of our brain architecture, which is inherited..."

Four weeks later, my period still hadn't arrived, and that was very weird; I had always been as regular as clockwork. But I knew that stress could mess up the cycle, and the combination of moving away from home, eating and sleeping at weird hours for weeks and then starting college was probably more than enough. But two weeks later it still hadn't come, and I was starting to have weird feelings that might be psychosomatic, but might not. So I bought a pregnancy test kit, and soon no doubt was left: I was pregnant, despite the impossibility of it. My gynecologist confirmed the home test with one of his own, and insisted that I must be less regular than I thought, or had miscounted, or both; there's just no way you could get pregnant from one sex act immediately after your period. It must have been spotting, not true menstruation; sperm just can't live in your Fallopian tubes for two weeks.

But I knew they had. And I knew that despite my doctor's offer to refer me to a trustworthy abortion clinic, and despite the uproar it would cause in my family, and despite the huge burden a baby would inflict on a teenage university student, that I was going to keep him. Somehow, even then, I

238

Nephil

knew it would be a boy. And somehow, I didn't panic
despite ample provocation; I weathered my mother's
lugubrious moaning and my father's angry shouting with
quiet aplomb, and reminded them that I was a legal adult who
was no longer economically dependent on them. My refusal
to accept this as the end of the world seemed to be
contagious, and by the time I actually started to show they
seemed almost happy about it. Happier than I was, in fact;
though I wasn't as miserable as an unwed mother was
expected to be back then, neither was I suffused with an aura
of impending Madonnahood. I simply couldn't see the
pregnancy as life-changing, either for good or ill.

Of course, I was wrong; having a totally helpless
human being in one's care is a lot bigger responsibility than
owning a dog. Luckily, my friends were steadfast; they
wouldn't hear any talk of my making other arrangements, so
Jason had two auxiliary mommies for his first year. After
that, Theresa got married and of course moved out; Jill stuck
with me until she, too, graduated, and our landlady was kind
enough to slightly decrease my rent until I could secure a
research fellowship to finance the next stage of my
education. That, too, was a direct result of my pregnancy, or
rather of the circumstances attending it; when I enrolled I had
absolutely no real idea what I wanted to study, but I became
so fascinated by what had happened to me that I wanted to
know all I could about it. In fact, it seemed to come naturally
to me; I was so obsessed with divining the secrets of
reproduction, most of it was more like a personal quest than
assigned study.

Jason did his part from the very beginning, by being a
perfect baby who grew into a model child. He rarely cried,

Ladies of the Night

even when given ample reason; I had no problems nursing him, and it was always easy to find sitters because he was always quiet. Most of the professors who knew us even let me bring him to class; as one of them quipped, "He's less trouble than some of the students and most of the faculty." Once he started preschool it got even easier; though he was a quiet, thoughtful child he was by no means an introvert, and got along famously with all the other children. He excelled equally at schoolwork, recess and keeping himself occupied; in fact, his second-grade teacher declared him the most adaptable student she had ever encountered in over thirty years of teaching.

That adaptability only became more pronounced as he grew older. His store of self-taught knowledge was immense, and he often spent hours or even days virtually alone (while I was immersed in some project or another) without complaint; yet, when he was among other people of any age he was gregarious and socially adept, and seemed to have the gift of keeping up an interesting conversation with anyone, from any background. Though it is true that he seemed to have inherited all of his physical characteristics from the maternal line, I couldn't help but notice that he had obviously inherited much of his father's personality.

"...But again, that behavior is shared between *all* humans, so it would be the same no matter *who* your father was."

"So you're saying I couldn't have inherited my father's personality?"

"No, I'm not saying that; what I'm saying is that your personality is the result of many complex factors, some of which may indeed have been inherited from your father."

240

Nephil

"But hypothetically, extremely complex behaviors and knowledge, more complex than any seen in any known organism, could be transmitted in the genes."

"I suppose so, provided the genome was large enough."

"Or efficient enough. There's a tremendous amount of redundancy in the human genome."

I smiled. "I'm the one who taught you that, kiddo."

"But hypothetically, you could have, say, a genetically-engineered life form with a genome no bigger than a human's, yet encoded with a great deal more information. Maybe even a lot of complex behavior and inherited memory."

"Hypothetically, yes. But such a being wouldn't be able to mate with whatever creature you had engineered it from; the chromosomes wouldn't match up, even if they were similar in size and number."

The resemblance became ever-creepier as he got older. Though I had known Jim for only a few hours, his face, his voice, his behavior, in fact everything about him was indelibly impressed upon my memory like those of an old friend. And though it had been seventeen years, that memory - and truth be told, my feelings for him - were evergreen. Despite the fact that Jason looked absolutely nothing like his father, the resemblance of their personalities was uncanny; after his voice changed he even *sounded* like Jim. So when Jason displayed certain…peculiarities, I naturally couldn't help thinking that perhaps these were also things he had inherited from his father, things I had not had the time or opportunity to see.

Things like the fact that he only acted like Jim when he was around me; what I heard from others was often quite different, as though he were altering his personality to match that person's idea of an appealing young man, socially or sexually.

Things like the way he liked to sit for hours in the back yard, staring up at the stars, and could repeat all sorts of facts about them, including things I couldn't find in any reference book that he couldn't tell me how he knew.

Things like the fact that he had literally never been sick a single day in his life, not even as much as a sniffle or tummyache. Not even a bruise. Not even a cut or scrape. Not even a sprain the time he fell twenty feet from the roof while trying to fly.

Not even a lost tooth; the deciduous ones seemed to be seamlessly replaced by adult ones as he grew, as if by magic. I never told anyone because I knew they wouldn't believe me, any more than they had believed my pregnancy had been impossible by all the known laws of biology. The search for the secret of what Jim had done to me, and what he had bequeathed to the son he had sired, grew from a quest into an obsession, and produced a PhD almost as a side-effect. I searched diligently in the literature, but never found anything that could explain the central mystery of my life and my son's existence: *What in God's name was Jim? And how much was Jason really like his father?*

He quietly placed a slim library-bound volume on the table. I didn't need to look to know its identity. *"Genetic*

Nephil

Malleability: A Hypothetical Model for Reproduction in Astropelagic Species," he read aloud.

"That was just an intellectual game, as you know if you read it; I was trying to come up with a feasible explanation for how some aliens might conceivably mate with humans as they do so often in sci-fi, and why such a mechanism might have evolved in the first place."

"A pretty serious game; this represents at least five or six years of research."

"Eight," I said quietly.

"I like your neologism 'astropelagic'. The outer-space equivalent of animals which live out their lives in the deep ocean, far from the sight of land."

"Yes."

"Except when it's time to spawn."

I nodded weakly. "I reasoned that given the vast distances of interstellar space, such creatures would need a means of reproducing with any convenient female. That would mean not only fooling her into thinking he was a male of her own species and inducing her to mate in a relatively short time, but also having the ability to rearrange his chromosomal structure to match hers well enough to fool her cellular machinery."

"Since his own mother would've been of a different species entirely, most of the information for the son's juvenile form would be inherited from the mother. And in order to continue the life-cycle of his kind, he'd need to inherit certain behaviors and considerable knowledge from his father."

Ladies of the Night

There was an extremely long pause, of the sort bad writers term "pregnant". Then I said, "It's all just hypothetical."

He put his hand on mine and said, in a tone belying his youth, "I think we both know better."

He held me for a very long time while I cried; it struck me that I had never once had to do the same for him. But eventually, the tears came to a stop, and I was able to choke out the question: "When will you be leaving?"

"I don't know, Mom. Pretty soon, though, I think. It's just a kind of urge, an instinct. But it's been getting stronger for the past few months; I don't think I'll be able to resist it much longer."

"Like a salmon leaving its spawning pond to head down to the sea."

"Yes."

"Salmon come back to the same pond when it's time for them to spawn."

"We don't."

"Then I'll never see you again?" I had to struggle to ask.

"No." It was a plain statement of fact. And then I dissolved into tears again, and he held me for a long time while the only world I would ever know turned beneath the distant stars to which he belonged.

About the Author

Maggie McNeill was a librarian in suburban New Orleans, but after divorce economic necessity spurred her to take up sex work; from 1997 to 2006 she worked first as a stripper, then as a call girl and madam. She eventually married her favorite client, retired, and moved to a ranch in the rural Upper South. There she writes a daily blog called "The Honest Courtesan" (http://maggiemcneill.wordpress.com/) which examines the realities, myths, history, lore, science, philosophy, art, and every other aspect of prostitution; she also reports sex work news, critiques the way her profession is treated in the media and by governments, and is frequently consulted by academics and journalists as an expert on the subject.

Made in the USA
San Bernardino, CA
27 March 2016